Hearts Afire
Marta Perry

Steeple Hill®

Published by Steeple Hill Books™

STEEPLE HILL BOOKS

Steeple
Hill®

ISBN-13: 978-0-373-87416-3
ISBN-10:   0-373-87416-2

HEARTS AFIRE

Therefore we also, since we are surrounded by so great a cloud of witnesses, let us lay aside every weight, and the sin which so easily ensnares us, and let us run with endurance the race that is set before us.

—*Hebrews* 12:1

Chapter One

Terry Flanagan flashed a penlight in the young boy's eyes and then smiled reassuringly at the teenage sister who was riding with them in the rig on the trip to the hospital.

"You can hit the siren," she called through the narrow doorway to her partner. Jeff Erhart was driving the unit this run. They had an unspoken agreement that she'd administer care when the patient was a small child. With three young kids of his own, Jeff found a hurt child tough to face.

The sister's dark gaze focused on Terry. "Why did you tell him to start the siren? Is Juan worse? Tell me!"

"He's going to be fine, Manuela." She'd agreed to take the sister in the unit because she was the only family member who spoke English. "You have to stay calm, remember?" Naturally it was scary for Manuela to see her little brother immobilized on a backboard, an IV running into his arm.

The girl swallowed hard, nodding. With her dark hair pulled back in braids and her skin innocent of makeup, Manuela didn't look the sixteen years she claimed to be.

Possibly she was sixteen only because that was the minimum age for migrant farmworkers to be in the fields. The fertile farmlands and orchards that surrounded the small city of Suffolk in southern Pennsylvania were a magnet for busloads of migrant farmworkers, most from Mexico, who visited the area for weeks at a time. They rarely intersected with the local community except in an emergency, like this one.

"Juan will need stitches, yes?" Manuela clasped her little brother's hand.

"Yes, he will." Terry lifted the gauze pad slightly. The bleeding had slowed, but the edges of the cut gaped.

The child looked up at her with such simple trust that her stomach clenched. *Lord, I haven't forgotten anything, have I? Be with this child, and guide my hands and my decisions.*

She ticked over the steps of care as the unit hit the busy streets of Suffolk and slowed. She'd been over them already, but somehow she couldn't help doing it again. And again.

She knew why. It had been two years, but she still heard that accusing voice at moments like this, telling her that she was incompetent, that she—

No. She wouldn't go there. She'd turn the self-doubt over to God, as she'd done so many times before, and she'd close the door on that cold voice. The wail of the siren, the well-equipped emergency unit, the trim khaki pants and navy shirt with the word Paramedic emblazoned on the back—all those things assured her of who she was.

She smiled at the girl again, seeing the strain in her young face. "How did your brother get hurt? Can you tell me that?"

"He shouldn't have been there." The words burst out. "He's too little to—"

The child's fingers closed over hers, as if he understood what she was saying. A look flashed between brother and sister, too quickly for Terry to be sure what it meant. A warning? Perhaps.

She could think of only one ending to what Manuela had started to say. "Was Juan working in the field?" It was illegal for a child so young to work in the fields—everyone knew that, even those who managed to ignore the migrant workers in their midst every summer and fall.

Alarm filled the girl's eyes. "I didn't say that. You can't tell anyone I said that!"

The boy, catching his sister's emotion, clutched her hand tightly and murmured something in Spanish. His eyes were huge in his pinched, pale face.

Compunction flooded Terry. She couldn't let the child become upset. "It's okay," she said, patting him gently. "Manuela, tell your brother everything is okay. I misunderstood, that's all."

Manuela nodded, bending over her brother, saying something in a soft voice. Terry watched, frowning. Something was going on there—something the girl didn't want her to pursue.

She glanced out the window. They were making the turn into the hospital driveway. This wasn't over. Once they were inside, she'd find out how the child had been injured, one way or another.

Jeff cut the siren and pulled to a stop. By the time she'd opened the back doors, he was there to help her slide the stretcher smoothly out.

They rolled boy and stretcher quickly through the automatic doors and into the hands of the waiting E.R. team.

Terry flashed a grin at Harriet Conway. With her brown hair pulled back and her oversized glasses, Harriet might look severe, but Terry knew and respected her. The hospital had been afloat with rumors about the new head of emergency medicine, but no one seemed to know yet who it was. All they knew was that the new appointment probably meant change, and nobody liked change.

She reported quickly, in the shorthand that developed between people who liked and trusted each other. Harriet nodded, clipping orders as they wheeled the boy toward a treatment room. This was usually the paramedic's cue to stay behind, unless the E.R. was shorthanded, but Terry was reluctant.

She bent over the child. "This is Dr. Conway, Juan. She's going to take good care of you."

She looked around for Manuela, and found the girl near the door, her arms around her mother. Two men stood awkwardly to the side, clearly uncomfortable with the woman's tears. One, the father, turned a hat in work-worn hands, the knees of his work pants caked with mud from kneeling in the tomato field.

The other man was the crew chief, Mel Jordan. He'd driven Mr. and Mrs. Ortiz. He'd know if Juan had been working in the field when he was injured, but he wouldn't want to admit it.

Manuela came back to the stretcher in a rush, repeating Terry's words to her little brother. Taking in the situation, Harriet jerked her head toward the exam room.

"Looks like you'd both better come in."

Good. Terry pushed the stretcher through the

swinging door. Because she didn't intend to leave until she knew what had happened to the child.

The next few minutes had to be as difficult for the sister as they were for the patient, but Manuela hung in there like a trouper, singing to Juan and teasing a smile out of him.

Finally the wound was cleaned, the stitches in, and Harriet straightened with a smile. "Okay, good job, young man. You're going to be fine, but you be more careful next time."

Manuela translated, and Juan managed another smile.

Harriet headed for the door. "I'll send the parents in now. Thanks, Terry."

This was probably her only chance to find out what had really happened at the camp. She leaned across the bed to clasp Manuela's hand.

"How was your brother hurt? What happened to him?"

Manuela's eyes widened. "I don't understand."

She bit back frustration. "I think you do. I want to know how your little brother cut his head. Was he working in the field?"

"What are you trying to pull?"

Terry swung around. The crew chief stood in the door, Dr. Conway and the anxious parents behind him.

"No kid works in the field. It's against the law. You think I don't know that?" Inimical eyes in a puffy, flushed face glared at her. Jordan had the look of a man who drank too much, ate unwisely and would clog his arteries by fifty if he had his way.

Dr. Conway pushed past him, letting the parents sidle into the room with her. "What's up, Terry? Is there some question about how the boy was hurt?"

"I'd like to be sure." Ignoring the crew chief, she focused on Manuela, who was talking to her parents. "Manuela, what was your little brother doing when he was hurt?"

Manuela's father said something short and staccato in Spanish, his dark eyes opaque, giving away nothing. How much of this had he understood? Why hadn't she taken Spanish in high school, instead of the German for which she'd never found a use?

There was a flash of rebellion in Manuela's face. Then she looked down, eyes masked by long, dark lashes.

"He was playing. He fell and hit his head on a rock. That's all."

She was lying, Terry was sure of it. "When we were in the ambulance, you said—"

"The girl answered you." The crew chief shoved his bulky figure between Terry and the girl. "Let's get going." He added something in Spanish, and the father bent to pick up the boy.

"Wait a minute. You can't leave yet." They were going to walk out, and once that happened, she'd have no chance to get to the truth, no chance to fix things for that hurt child.

"We're going, and you can't keep the kid here."

The mother, frightened, burst into speech. Her husband and Manuela tried to soothe her. The boy began to cry.

Terry glanced to Dr. Conway in a silent plea for backup. But Harriet was looking past her, toward the open door of the exam room.

"What's the problem here?" An incisive voice cut through the babble of voices. "This is a hospital, people."

"The new E.R. chief," Harriet murmured to Terry, the faintest flicker of an eyelid conveying a warning.

Terry didn't need the warning. She knew who was there even before her mind had processed the information, probably because that voice had already seared her soul. Slowly she turned.

She hadn't imagined it. Dr. Jacob Landsdowne stood glaring at her. Six feet of frost with icicle eyes, some wit at Philadelphia General had once called him. It still fit.

He gave no sign that he recognized her, though he must. She hadn't changed in two years, except to gain about ten years of experience. Those icy blue eyes touched her and dismissed her as he focused on Harriet.

Harriet took her time consulting the chart in her hand before answering him. Terry knew her friend well enough to know that was deliberate—Harriet letting him know this was her turf.

Well, good. Harriet would need every ounce of confidence she possessed to hold her own against Jake Landsdowne.

Harriet gave him a quick précis of Juan's condition and treatment, giving Terry the chance to take a breath.

Steady. Don't panic. You haven't done anything wrong.

"The paramedic questions how the child was injured," Harriet concluded. "I was about to pursue that when you came in." She nodded toward Terry. "Terry Flanagan, Suffolk Fire Department."

She couldn't have extended her hand if her life depended on it. It didn't matter, since the great Dr. Landsdowne wouldn't shake hands with a mere paramedic. He gave a curt nod and turned to the group clustered around the child.

"The kiddo's folks don't speak English, Doc." The crew chief was all smiles now, apparently smart enough to realize his bluster wouldn't work with Landsdowne. "Manuela here was saying that the little one fell and cut his head. Shame, but just an accident."

She wouldn't believe the man any farther than she could throw him, but Landsdowne's face registered only polite attention. He looked at Manuela. "Is that correct?"

Manuela's gaze slid away from his. "Yes, sir."

"Then I think we're done here. Dr. Conway, I'll leave you to sign the patient out." He turned and was gone before Terry found wits to speak.

Quickly, before she could lose the courage, she followed him to the hall. "Dr. Landsdowne—"

He stopped, frowning at her as if she were some lower species of life that had unaccountably found its way into his Emergency Room. "Well?"

She tried to blot out the memory of their last encounter. "While we were en route, I got the impression there might be more to this. If the child was injured while working in the field—"

"Did anyone say that?"

"Not in so many words."

"Then the hospital has no right to interfere. And neither do you."

He couldn't turn his back on her fast enough. He swept off with that long lope that seemed to cover miles of hospital corridor.

That settled that, apparently. She looked after the retreating figure.

Jake Landsdowne had changed more than she'd have expected in the past two years. He still had those steely blue eyes and the black hair brushed back from an angled, intelligent face, that faintly supercilious air that went along with a background of wealth and standing in the medical community.

But his broad shoulders appeared to carry a heavy burden, and those lines of strain around his eyes and mouth hadn't been there when she'd known him.

What was he doing here, anyway? She could only be surprised that she hadn't thought of that question sooner.

Jacob Landsdowne III had been a neurosurgery resident in Philadelphia two years ago, known to the E.R. staff and a lowly paramedic only because he'd been the neurosurgery consult called to the E.R. He'd been on the fast track, everyone said, the son of a noted neurosurgeon, being groomed to take over his father's practice, top ten percent of his med school class, dating a Main Line socialite who could only add to his prestige.

Now he was a temporary Chief of Emergency Services at a small hospital in a small city in rural Pennsylvania. She knew, only too well, what had happened to the socialite. But what had happened to Jake?

He'd changed. But one thing hadn't changed. He still stared at Terry Flanagan with contempt in his face.

"Glad you could join us, Dr. Landsdowne." Sam Getz, Providence Hospital's Chief of Staff, didn't look glad. *Let's see how you measure up,* that's what his expression always said when he looked at Jake.

"I appreciate the opportunity to meet with the board." He nodded to the three people seated around the polished mahogany table in the conference room high above the patient care areas of the hospital.

A summons to the boardroom was enough to make any physician examine his conduct, but Getz had merely said the board's committee for community outreach was considering a project he might be interested in. Given the fact that Jake's contract was for a six-month trial period, he was bound to be interested in anything the board wanted him to do.

Last chance, a voice whispered in his head. *Last chance to make it as a physician. They all know that.*

Did they? He might be overreacting. He helped himself to a mug of coffee, gaining a moment to get his game face on.

Getz knew his history, but the elderly doctor didn't seem the sort to gossip. In fact, Sam Getz looked like nothing so much as one of the Pennsylvania Dutch farmers Jake had seen at the local farmer's market, with his square, ruddy face and those bright blue eyes.

Dr. Getz tapped on the table, and Jake slid into the nearest chair like a tardy student arriving after the lecture had begun. "Time to get started, folks." He nodded toward the door, where two more people were entering. "You all know Pastor Flanagan, our fellow board member. And this is his cousin, Paramedic Terry Flanagan. They have something to say to the board."

Good thing his coffee was in a heavy mug. If he'd held a foam cup, it would have been all over the table. Terry Flanagan. Was she here to lodge a complaint against him?

Common sense won out. Terry would hardly bring up that painful incident, especially not to the community outreach committee. This had to be about something else.

The other people seated around the table were flipping open the folders that had been put at each place.

He opened his gingerly, to find a proposal for Providence Hospital to establish a clinic to serve migrant farmworkers.

He pictured Terry, bending over the migrant child in the E.R., protectiveness in every line of her body. Was that what this was about?

He'd been so shocked to see her that he'd handled the situation on autopilot. He'd read equal measure of shock in her face at the sight of him. What were the chances that they'd bump up against one another again?

He yanked his thoughts from that, focusing on the minister. Pastor Flanagan spoke quickly, outlining the needs of the migrant workers and the efforts his church was making. So he was both Terry's cousin and a member of the board—that was an unpleasant shock.

This was what she'd done then, after the tragedy. She'd run home. At the time, he'd neither known nor cared what had become of her. He'd simply wanted her away from his hospital. Not that it had stayed his hospital for long.

The minister ended with a plea for the board to consider their proposal, and Terry stood to speak. Her square, capable hands trembled slightly on the folder until she pressed them against the tabletop.

Had she changed, in the past two years? He couldn't decide. Probably he'd never have noticed her, in that busy city E.R., if it hadn't been for her mop of red curls, those fierce green eyes, and the air of determination warring with the naiveté in her heart-shaped face.

That was what had changed, he realized. The naiveté was gone. Grim experience had rubbed the innocence off the young paramedic.

The determination was still there. Even though her audience didn't give her much encouragement, her voice grew impassioned, and the force of her desire to help wrung a bit of unwilling admiration from him. She knew her stuff, too—knew how many migrant workers came through in a season, how many children, what government programs were in place to help.

William Morley, the hospital administrator, shifted uneasily in his chair as her presentation came to a close. His fingers twitched as if he added up costs.

"What you say may be true," he said. "But why can't those people simply come to the emergency room? Or call the paramedics?"

"They'll only call the paramedics in case of dire emergency." Terry leaned forward, her nervousness obviously forgotten in her passion. "Too many migrants are afraid of having contact—afraid their papers aren't in order or they're simply afraid of authority. As for the E.R., no one from the migrant camps comes in unless it's a case where the police or the paramedics become involved. They're afraid, and they're also dependent on the crew chief for transportation."

Jake heard what she didn't say. He hadn't thought too highly of the unctuous crew chief, either. But would he really refuse to transport someone who needed care? And did Terry, in spite of her enthusiasm, have the skills necessary to manage a job like this? He doubted it.

Morley was already shaking his head, the overhead light reflecting from it. If he'd grown that pencil-thin moustache to compensate for his baldness, it wasn't working. "Starting a clinic isn't the answer. Let the government handle the situation. We do our part by accepting the cases in the E.R. And, might I add, we are rarely paid anything."

"That's a point." A board member whose name escaped Jake leaned forward, tapping his pen on the table for emphasis. "We'd put ourselves at risk with a clinic. What about insurance coverage? When they come to the E.R., we have backups and safeguards. If Ms. Flanagan or one of her volunteers made a mistake, we'd be liable."

He thought Terry's cheeks paled a little at that comment, but she didn't back down. "The hospital can establish any protocol it wishes for treatment. And I plan to recruit staff from among the medical professionals right in our community."

"How many people do you think have the time to do that?" Morley's head went back and forth in what seemed his characteristic response to any risk. "Really, Ms. Flanagan, I don't see how you can make this work in such a short time. Perhaps in another year—"

The mood of the board was going against her, Jake sensed. Well, he couldn't blame them. They didn't want to take a chance. He understood that.

"I have several volunteers signed up from my congregation," Pastor Flanagan said. "And I've spoken with the owner of Dixon Farms, the largest employer of migrant workers in the county."

"You're not going to tell me old Matthew Dixon agreed to help." Dr. Getz spoke for the first time, and Jake realized he'd been waiting—for what, Jake couldn't guess. "The man still has the first dollar he ever made."

If the minister agreed, he didn't show it. "He'll allow us to establish the clinic on his property. There's even a building we can use."

"If you can sell this idea to Matt Dixon, Pastor, you're wasted in the ministry. You should be in sales." Getz chuckled at his own joke, and Pastor Flanagan smiled weakly.

"That hardly solves the problem of liability," Morley said. "No, no, I'm afraid this just won't do. We can't—"

Getz interrupted with a gesture. "I have a solution that will satisfy everyone." The fact that Morley fell silent and sat back in his chair told Jake volumes about the balance of power in this particular hospital. "We need a volunteer from our own medical staff to head up the clinic. That's all." He turned toward Jake, still smiling. "I'm sure Dr. Landsdowne would be willing to volunteer."

Silence, dead silence. Jake stared at him, appalled. He could think of a hundred things that could go wrong in an operation like this, and any one of them could backfire on him, ending his last hope for a decent career. He had every reason in the world to say no, but one over-riding reason to say yes. He had no choice. This wasn't voluntary, and he and Getz both knew it.

He straightened, trying to assume an expression of enthusiasm. "Of course, I'd be happy to take this on. Assuming Ms. Flanagan is willing to work with me, naturally."

Terry looked as appalled as he felt, but she had no more choice than he did. "Yes." She clipped off the word. "Fine."

"That's settled, then." Getz rubbed his palms. "Good. I like it when everything comes together this way. Well, ladies and gentlemen, I think we're adjourned."

Chairs scraped as people rose. Jake glanced at Terry, his gaze colliding with hers. She flushed, but she didn't look away. Her mouth set in a stubborn line that told him he was in for a fight.

He didn't mind a fight, but one thing he was sure of. Terry Flanagan and her clinic couldn't be allowed to throw him off course toward his goal. No matter what he had to do to stop her.

Chapter Two

"It's not the best thing that ever happened to me, that's for sure." Terry slumped into the chair across from Harriet in the E.R. lounge a few days later, responding to her friend's question about working with Jake Landsdowne. "It looks as if he's not any more eager to supervise the clinic than I am to have him. He hasn't been in touch with me at all."

Actually, she was relieved at that, although she could hardly say so. She'd tensed every time the phone had rung, sure it would be him.

"That's too bad. How are you going to make any progress if Dr. Landsdowne won't cooperate?"

Terry shrugged. "I've gone ahead without him."

"I'm not sure that's such a good idea." Harriet frowned down at her coffee mug. "He's very much a hands-on chief. He's been shaking up the E.R., let me tell you."

"I'm sorry." But not surprised. Jake Landsdowne had always been supremely confident that his way was the best way. The only way, in fact.

Harriet shrugged. "I expected it. Just be careful with him. I know how much this clinic means to you. You don't want to put the project in jeopardy by antagonizing the man."

Terry thought of Juan's frightened face, of the suppressed anger she'd sensed in Manuela. Of the other children she'd glimpsed on her trip to the migrant camp.

"I'll be careful." She had more reason than most to know she had to tread carefully. For a moment the need to confide in Harriet about her past experience with Jake almost overwhelmed her caution.

Almost, but not quite. She had to watch her step.

Please, Father, help me to guard my tongue. Telling Harriet would put her in an impossible position, and it wouldn't be fair to Jake, either. I just wish You'd show me a clear path through this situation.

"Did you know Dr. Landsdowne when you worked in Philadelphia? You must have been there at about the same time."

Harriet's question shook her. She hadn't realized that anyone would put the two things together, but naturally Harriet would be interested in her new boss's record.

"I knew him slightly," she said carefully. She wouldn't lie, but she didn't have to spell out all the details, either. "Mostly by reputation."

Anybody's life could be fodder for hospital gossip, and the handsome, talented neurosurgery resident had been a magnet for it. Still—

"Excuse me."

Terry spun, nerves tensing. How long had Jake been standing in the doorway? How much had he heard?

"Dr. Landsdowne." Harriet's tone was cool. Clearly

Jake hadn't convinced her yet that he deserved to be her superior.

"I heard Ms. Flanagan was here." The ice in his voice probably meant that he knew she'd been talking about him. "I'm surprised you haven't been here before this. We need to talk about this clinic proposal."

Not a proposal, she wanted to say. It's been approved, remember?

Still, that hardly seemed the way to earn his cooperation. "Do you have time to discuss it now?"

He nodded. "Come back to my office." He turned and walked away, clearly expecting her to follow.

She'd rather talk on neutral ground in the lounge, but she wasn't given a choice. She shrugged in response to Harriet's sympathetic smile and followed him down the corridor. All she wanted was to get this interview over as quickly as possible.

The office consisted of four hospital-green walls and a beige desk. Nothing had been done to make it Jake's except for the nameplate on the desk. Maybe that was what he wanted.

He stalked to the desk, picked up a file folder, and thrust it at her. "Here are the regulations we've come up with for the clinic. You'll want to familiarize yourself with them."

She held the folder, not opening it. "We?"

His frown deepened. "Mr. Morley, the hospital administrator, wanted to have some input."

She could imagine the sort of input Morley would provide, with his fear of doing anything that might result in a lawsuit. Well, that was his job, she supposed. She flipped open the folder, wondering just how bad it was going to be.

In a moment she knew. She snapped the folder shut. "This makes it practically impossible for my volunteers to do anything without an explicit order from a doctor."

"Both Mr. Morley and I feel that we can't risk letting volunteers, trained or not, treat patients without the approval of the physician in charge."

"You, in other words."

"That's correct." His eyebrows lifted. "You agreed to the terms, as I recall."

"I didn't expect them to be so stringent. My people are all medical professionals—I don't have anyone with less than an EMT-3 certification. You're saying you don't trust them to do anything without your express direction."

Were they talking about her volunteers? Or her?

"You can give all the sanitation and nutrition advice you want. I'm sure that will be appreciated. Anything else, and—"

His condescending tone finally broke through her determination to play it safe with him. "Are you taking it out on the program because you blame me for Meredith Stanley's death?"

She'd thought the name often enough since Jake's arrival. She just hadn't expected to say it aloud. Or to feel the icy silence that greeted it.

For a long moment he stared at her—long enough for her to regret her hasty words, long enough to form a frantic prayer for wisdom. "I'm sorry. I shouldn't have said that."

"No. You shouldn't." His face tightened with what might have been either grief or bitterness. He turned away, seeming to buy a moment's respite by walking to the window that looked out over the hospital parking lot. Then he swung back to face her. "What happened two years ago has nothing to do with the clinic." The words were clipped, cutting. "I think it best if we both try to forget the past."

Could he really do that? Forget the suicide of a woman who'd said she loved him? Forget blaming the paramedics who'd tried to save her? Forget the gossip that said he was the one at fault?

Maybe he could. But she never would.

He seemed to take her assent for granted. He nodded toward the folder in her hands. "Read through that, discuss it with your volunteers. Possibly we can arrange for the clinic to be in phone or radio contact with the E.R. when it's open. We'll discuss that later."

"Yes." Her fingers clenched the manila folder so tightly someone would probably have to pry it loose. All she wanted now was to get away from him—as far away as possible.

He picked up a ring of keys from the desk. "Suppose we go out and look at this clinic of yours."

"Not now." The words came out instinctively. "I mean…we can schedule that at your convenience."

His eyebrows lifted again. "Now is convenient. Would you like to ride with me?"

She didn't even want to be in the same state with him. "No. Thank you, but I'll need my car. Why don't you follow me out? The camp is a little tricky to find."

If she were fortunate, maybe he'd get lost on the maze of narrow country roads that led to the migrant compound. But somehow, she didn't think that was likely to happen.

* * *

Jake kept Terry's elderly sedan in sight as they left the outskirts of Suffolk and started down a winding country road. He hadn't gotten used to the fact that the area went so quickly from suburbs to true country, with fields of corn and soybeans stretching along either side of the road.

He frowned at the back of her head, red curls visible as she leaned forward to adjust something—the radio, probably. He shouldn't have been so harsh with her. It wasn't Terry's fault that he couldn't see her now without picturing her racing the stretcher into the E.R., without seeing Meredith's blank, lifeless face, without being overwhelmed with guilt.

Just let me be a doctor again. That's all I ask. I'll save other lives. Isn't that worth something?

And did he really believe saving others would make up for failing Meredith? His jaw tightened. Nothing would make up for that. Maybe that was why God stayed so silent when he tried to pray.

Meredith's death wasn't Terry's fault. But if someone more experienced had taken the call—if he had checked his messages earlier—if, if, if. No amount of what-ifs could change the past. Could change his culpability.

He pushed it from his mind. Concentrate on now. That means making sure Terry and her clinic don't derail your future.

It was farther than he'd expected to the Dixon Farms. The route wound past rounded ridges dense with forest and lower hills crowned by orchards, their trees heavy with fruit. Finally Terry turned onto a gravel road. An abundant supply of No Trespassing signs informed him that they were on Dixon Farms property. Apparently, Matthew Dixon had strong feelings about outsiders.

He gritted his teeth as the car bottomed out in a rut. Surely there was a better way to provide health care for the migrant workers. Wouldn't it make more sense to bring the workers to health care, instead of trying to bring health care to them? If Dr. Getz had given him any idea of what he'd been walking into that day at the board meeting, he'd have been prepared with alternatives.

Terry bounced to a stop next to several other vehicles in a rutted field. He drove up more slowly, trying to spare his car the worst of the ruts. Not waiting for him, she walked toward a cement block building that must be the site for the clinic. It was plopped down at the edge of a field. Beyond it, a strip of woods stretched up the shoulder of the ridge.

He parked and slid out. If he could find some good reason why this facility wasn't suitable, maybe they could still go back and revisit the whole idea. Find a way of dealing with the problem that wouldn't put the hospital at so much risk. To say nothing of the risk to what was left of his career.

Several people moved in and around the long, low, one-story building. Terry had obviously recruited volunteers already. The more people involved, the harder it would be to change.

Pastor Brendan Flanagan straightened at his approach, turning off the hose he was running. "Welcome. I'd offer to shake hands, but I'm way too dirty. I'm glad you're here, Dr. Landsdowne."

"Jake, please, Pastor."

"And I'm Brendan to all but the most old-fashioned of my parishioners." The minister, in cutoff jeans, sneakers and a Phillies T-shirt, didn't look much like he had at the board meeting.

"Brendan." Jake glanced around, spotting five or six people working. "What are you up to?"

"We recruited a few people to get the place in shape. Dixon hasn't used it for anything but storage in a couple of decades." He nodded toward what appeared to be a pile of broken farm implements. "It'll be ready soon. Don't worry about that."

That wasn't what he was worried about, but he wasn't going to confide in the minister. "I'll have a look inside."

He stooped a little, stepping through the door. The farmer certainly hadn't parted with anything of value when he'd donated this space.

"You must be Dr. Landsdowne." The woman who had been brushing the walls down with a broom stopped, extending her hand to him. "I'm Siobhan Flanagan."

"Another Flanagan?" He couldn't help but ask. The woman had dark hair, slightly touched with gray, and deep blue eyes that seemed to contain a smile.

"Another one, I'm afraid. I'm Terry's mother. Brendan recruited me to lend a hand today." She gestured around the large, rectangular room, its floors pockmarked and dirty, its few windows grimy. "I know it doesn't look like much yet, but just wait until we're done. You won't know the place."

He might be able to tell Terry the place was a hovel, but he could hardly say that to the woman who smiled with such enthusiasm. "You must look at the world through rose-colored glasses, Mrs. Flanagan."

"Isn't that better than seeing nothing but the thorns, Dr. Landsdowne?"

He held up his hands in surrender. "I'll take your word for it." She'd made him smile, and he realized how seldom that happened recently.

Somehow the place didn't seem quite as dismal as it had a moment ago. It reminded him of the clinic in Somalia. For an instant he heard the wails of malnourished children, felt the oppressive heat smothering him, sensed the comradeship that blossomed among people fighting impossible odds.

He shook off the memories. That was yet another place he'd failed.

Through the open doorway, he spotted the red blaze of Terry's hair. She was in the process of confronting an elderly man whose fierce glare should have wilted her. It didn't seem to be having that effect.

He went toward them quickly, in time to catch a few words.

"...now, Mr. Dixon, you can see perfectly well that we're not harming your shed in any way."

"Is there a problem?" Jake stopped beside her.

The glare turned on him. "I suppose you're that new doctor—the one that's in charge around here. Taking a man's property and making a mess of it."

This was Matthew Dixon, obviously. "I'm Dr. Landsdowne, yes. I understood from Pastor Flanagan that you agreed to the use of your building as a clinic. Isn't that right?" If the old man objected, that would be a perfect reason to close down the project.

"Oh, agree. Well, I suppose I did. When a man's minister calls on him and starts talking about what the Lord expects of him, he doesn't have much choice, does he?"

"If you've changed your mind—"

"Who says I've changed my mind? I just want to be sure things are done right and proper, that's all. I want to hear that from the man in charge, not from this chit of a girl."

He glimpsed the color come up in Terry's cheeks at that, and he had an absurd desire to defend her.

"Ms. Flanagan is a fully certified paramedic, but if you want to hear it from me, you certainly will. I assure you there won't be any problems here."

A car pulled up in a swirl of dust. The man who slid out seemed to take the situation in at a glance, and he sent Jake a look of apology. He was lean and rangy like the elder Dixon, with the same craggy features, but a good forty years younger.

"Dad, you're not supposed to be out here." He took Dixon's arm and tried to turn him toward the car. "Terry and the others have work to do." He winked at Terry, apparently an old friend. "Let's get you back to the house."

Dixon shook off his hand. "I'll get myself to the house when I'm good and ready. A man's got a right to see what's happening on his own property."

"Yes, but I promised you I'd take care of it, remember? You should be resting." The son eased the older man to the car and helped him get in, talking softly. Once Dixon was settled, he turned to them.

"Sorry about that. I'm afraid once Dad gets an idea in his head, it's tough to get it out. I'm Andrew Dixon, by the way. You'd be Dr. Landsdowne. And I know

Terry, of course." He put his arm around her shoulders. "She used to be my best girl."

Terry wiggled free, but the look she turned on the man was open and friendly—a far cry from the way she looked at him. "Back in kindergarten, I think that was. Good to see you, Andy."

"Listen, if you have any problems, come to me, not the old man. No point in worrying him."

"There won't be any problems." He hoped.

Andrew smiled and walked quickly toward the driver's side of the car, as if afraid his father would hop back out if he didn't hurry.

The elder Dixon rolled down his window. "You make sure everything's done right," he bellowed. "Anything else, and I'll shut you down, that's what I'll do."

Shaking his head, Andrew put the car in gear and pulled out, disappearing quickly down the lane, the dust settling behind the car.

Jake looked down at Terry. There were several things he'd like to say to her. He raised an eyebrow. "So, are you still his best girl?"

Her face crinkled with laughter. "Not since he took my yellow crayon."

He found himself smiling back, just as involuntarily as he had smiled at her mother. Her green eyes softened, the pink in her cheeks seeming to deepen. She had a dimple at the corner of her mouth that only appeared when her face relaxed in a smile.

These Flanagan women had a way of getting under his guard. Without thinking, he took a step closer to her.

And stopped.

I always told you your emotions would get the best

of you. His father's voice seemed to echo in his ears. *Now it's cost you your career.*

Not entirely. He still had a chance. But that chance didn't include anything as foolish as feeling attraction for anyone, especially not Terry Flanagan.

Terry took an instinctive step back—away from Jake, away from that surge of attraction. *Don't be stupid. Jake doesn't feel anything. It's just you, and a remnants of what you once thought you saw in him.*

She turned away to hide her confusion, her gaze falling on the trailer Brendan had managed to borrow from one of his parishioners. Bren never hesitated to approach anyone he thought had something to offer for good works.

"Would you like to see the equipment we have so far?" She was relieved to find her voice sounded normal. "It's stored in the trailer until we can get the building ready." She started toward the trailer, and he followed without comment.

She was fine. Just because she'd had a juvenile crush on him two years ago, didn't mean they couldn't relate as professionals now. After all, half the female staff at the hospital had had a crush on Jake. He'd never noticed any of them, as far as she could tell.

"It's locked, I hope?"

The question brought her back to the present in a hurry. She pulled the key from her pocket, showing him, and then unlocked the door. "We'll be very conscious of security, since the building is so isolated."

He nodded, grasping the door and pulling it open. "About meds, especially. All medications are to be kept in a locked box and picked up at the E.R. when clinic hours start and then returned with a complete drug list at the end of the day."

Naturally it was a sensible precaution, but didn't he think she'd figure that out without his telling her? Apparently not.

"This is what I've been able to beg or borrow so far. There are a few larger pieces, like desks and a filing cabinet, that we'll pick up when we're ready for them." She pulled the crumpled list from her jeans pocket and handed it to him.

He looked it over, frowning. What was he thinking? His silence made her nervous. Was he about to shut them down because they didn't have a fully equipped E.R. out here?

"I'm sure it looks primitive in comparison to what you're used to, but anything is better than what the workers have now."

"It looks fine," he said, handing the sheet back to her. "I've worked in worse."

She blinked. "You have?"

He leaned against the back of the trailer, looking down at her with a faint smile. "You sound surprised."

"Well, I thought—" She blundered to a stop. She could hardly ask him outright what had happened to his promising neurosurgery career.

"I didn't stay on in Philadelphia." Emotion clouded the deep blue of his eyes and then was gone. "I spent some time at a medical mission in Somalia."

She could only gape at him. Jacob Landsdowne III, the golden boy who'd seemed to have the world of medicine at his feet, working at an African mission? None of that fit what she remembered.

"That sounds fascinating." She managed to keep the surprise out of her voice, but he probably sensed it. "You must have seen a whole different world there—medically, I mean."

"In every way." The lines in his face deepened. "The challenges were incredible—heat, disease, sanitation, unstable political situation. And yet people did amazing work there."

She understood. That was the challenge that made her a paramedic, the challenge of caring for the sick and injured at the moment of crisis.

The emergency is over when you walk on the scene. That was what one of her instructors had drummed into them. No matter how bad it is, you have to make them believe that.

"You did good work there," she said softly, knowing it had to be true.

"A drop in the bucket, I'm afraid. There's so much need." He glanced at her, his eyebrows lifting. "Hardly the sort of job where you'd expect to find me, is it?"

"I didn't say that."

"You were thinking it."

"Yes, well—" They were getting dangerously close to the subject he'd already said he wouldn't talk about. "Everyone said you were headed straight toward a partnership with your father in neurosurgery."

"Everyone was wrong." Tense lines bracketed his mouth. "I found the challenges in Africa far more interesting."

There was more to it than that. There had to be, but he wouldn't tell her. How much of his change in direction had been caused by Meredith's death?

It had changed Terry's life. She'd given up her bid for independence and come running home to the safety of her family. Had he run, too?

Jake closed the doors and watched while she locked them, then reached out and double-checked.

She bit back a sigh. He couldn't even trust her to do something as simple as locking a door. How on earth were they going to run this clinic together?

Chapter Three

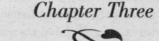

"Not a bad day, was it?" Terry glanced at her mother as they cleaned up after the clinic's opening day.

She probably should get over that need for Mom's approval. Most of her friends either called their mother by her first name and treated her like a girlfriend or else feigned complete contempt for anything a parent might think. She'd never been able to buy into either of those attitudes, maybe because Siobhan Flanagan never seemed to change.

Her mother turned from the cabinet where she was stacking clean linens. "No one would recognize this place from the way it looked a few short days ago. You can be proud of what you've accomplished."

Terry stared down at the meds she'd just finished counting and locked the drug box. She should be proud. But… "Three clients wasn't much for our first day, was it?"

"It will grow." Her mother's voice warmed. "Don't worry. People just have to learn to trust what's happening here. And they will."

"I hope so." It was one thing to charge into battle to help people and quite another to fear they didn't want your help at all. "Maybe I've leaped before I looked again." Her brothers had teased her mercilessly about that when she was growing up, especially when she'd tried to rope them into one of her campaigns to help a stray—animal or human.

"Don't you think that at all, Theresa Anne Flanagan. You've got a warm heart, and if that sometimes leads you into trouble, it's far better than armoring yourself like a—like an armadillo."

Terry grinned. "Do you have any particular armadillo in mind?"

Siobhan gave a rueful chuckle. "That was a mite unchristian, I guess. I'm trying to make up for it, though. I've invited Dr. Landsdowne to your brother's for the picnic on Sunday."

"You've what?" She could only hope her face didn't express the horror she felt. The Flanagan clan gathered for dinner most Sunday afternoons, and it wasn't unusual for someone to invite a friend. But Jake wasn't a friend—he was her boss, in a way, and also an antagonist. She wouldn't go so far as to think of him as an enemy, and she certainly didn't want to think of those moments when she'd felt, or imagined she'd felt, something completely inappropriate.

"What's wrong?" Her mother crossed to Terry, her face concerned. "I know you think he's a bit officious about the clinic, but if we get to know him better—"

"I already know him. From Philadelphia." Her throat tightened, and she had to force the words out. "He's the one I told you about. The one who blamed my team for the death of the woman he'd been seeing."

The words brought that time surging back, carrying a load of guilt, anxiety and the overwhelming fear that perhaps he'd been right. Perhaps she had been responsible.

"Oh, Terry, I didn't realize." Her mother gave her a quick, fierce hug. "I'm sorry."

She shook her head. "It's all right. I didn't tell anyone because—well, it didn't seem fair to me or to him."

Mom sat next to her on the desk. "Has he talked to you about it, since he's been here?"

"Only to say he thinks we should leave the past alone."

"But the inquiry cleared you of any wrongdoing. He should apologize, at least."

Terry's lips quirked at the thought of Jake apologizing. "He probably doesn't see it that way. Anyway, if anyone's guilty—" She stopped, regretting the words already.

Her mother just looked at her. Better people than she had crumbled at the force of that look.

"We'd been called to the woman's apartment before. Two or three times. Always the same thing—she'd taken an overdose of sleeping pills or tranquilizers. We figured out finally that she was being careful. Never taking enough to harm herself. Just enough to make people around her feel guilty."

"And Dr. Landsdowne was the person she wanted to feel guilty?"

She nodded, remembering the gossip that had flown around the hospital. "They'd been dating, but I guess when he wanted to break it off, she didn't take it very well." A brief image of Meredith flashed through her mind—tall, blond, elegant, the epitome of the Main

Line socialite. "I don't suppose anyone had ever turned her down before."

"Poor creature." Her mother's voice was warm with quick sympathy. "And him, too. What a terrible thing, to feel responsible for someone committing suicide. But what happened? You said she was careful."

"She took something she was allergic to." Terry's throat tightened with the memory. "We couldn't save her."

Her mother stroked Terry's hair the way she had when Terry had been a child, crying over a scraped knee. "That's probably why he blamed you. He couldn't face it."

Or because he did believe she was inept and incompetent. "I don't know, Mom." She pushed her hair back, suddenly tired. "I just know I've got to figure out how to deal with him now."

"Do you want me to cancel the invitation?" It was a testament to her mother's concern that she'd be willing to violate her sense of hospitality.

"No." She managed a smile. "I've got to get used to his presence. At least I'll be on my own turf there."

Her mother laughed. "And surrounded by Flanagans, all prepared to defend you."

"I don't need defending." The quick response was automatic. Her brothers had been trying to shelter her all her life. They'd never accept that she didn't need their protection.

"I know." Her mother gave her another hug and slid off the desk. "They mean well, sweetheart."

The sound of a horn turned Siobhan toward the door. "There's Mary Kate, coming for me. Are you heading for home now?"

"I just want to make one last check, okay?" And take a few minutes to clear her head. "I'll be right behind you."

"Walk out with me to say hi to your sister." Her mother linked her arm with Terry's.

Together they walked to where Mary Kate sat waiting. The back of her SUV was filled with grocery bags.

"Hi, Terry. Come on, Mom. I've got to get home before the frozen stuff melts."

"I'm ready." Siobhan slid into the car, while Terry leaned against the driver's side, scanning her big sister's face for signs of strain.

It had been ten months since Mary Kate lost her husband to a fast-moving cancer—ten months during which she kept up a brave face to the world, even to her own family.

"How're you doing? How are the kids?"

"Fine." Mary Kate's smile was a little too bright. "They're looking forward to seeing you on Sunday."

"Me, too." She wanted to say something—something meaningful, something that would help. But, as always, words faltered against Mary Kate's brittle facade. She'd never relax it, certainly not in front of her baby sister.

Terry stepped back, waving as the car disappeared in a cloud of dust down the lane. Then she walked back into the clinic, mind circling the question she knew her mother had wanted to ask. Why hadn't she told them the whole story about what happened in Philadelphia?

Because I was trying to prove I could accomplish something independent of my family. Because I failed.

Pointless, going over it and over it. She pushed herself into action, cleaning up the last few items that were out of place, locking the drug box, putting Jake's list of rules in the desk drawer. The cases that had come in today were so minor she hadn't even been tempted to bend any of the rules. Not that she would.

The door banged open. Manuela raced in. Terry's heart clutched at the look on her face.

"Manuela, what is it?"

The girl leaned against the desk, breathing hard. "Juan. He's sick. He's so hot. Please, you have to come." She grabbed Terry's arm in a desperate grasp. "Now. You have to come!"

Jake's rule flashed through her mind. Staff will not go to the migrant housing facility alone.

"I have to," she said aloud. "I have to." She grabbed her emergency kit and ran.

Manuela fled across the rutted field toward the back of the string of cement block buildings that served as dormitories for the workers. Terry struggled to keep up, mind churning. Juan's cut could have become infected. That seemed the most likely cause for a fever, but there were endless possibilities. If she had to take him to the hospital, she'd also have to explain how she'd come to break Jake's rules in her first day of operation.

The sun had already slid behind the ridge that overshadowed the camp. It would be nearly dark by the time she finished. She should have thought to bring a flashlight. She should have thought of a number of things, but it was too late now.

Please, Lord. Guide me and show me what must be done.

A snatch of guitar music, a burst of laughter, the

blare of a radio sounded from the far end of the camp. Words that she couldn't understand, cooking aromas that she couldn't identify—it was like being transported to a different country.

Manuela stopped to peer around the corner of the building, her finger to her lips to ensure Terry's silence. She didn't need to worry. Terry had no desire to draw attention to her presence.

But why was the girl so concerned with secrecy? If she'd fetched Terry without her parents' permission, that could be yet another complication to the rule she was already transgressing.

Manuela beckoned, and together they slipped around the corner and through the door. The room was a combination kitchen and living room, with a card table, a few straight chairs and a set of shelves against the wall holding plastic dishes and dented metal pots. An elderly woman, stirring something on a battered camp stove in the corner, stared at them incuriously and went back to her cooking.

Terry followed Manuela through a curtained door. At a guess, the whole family slept here on a motley collection of beds and cots jammed together. Juan lay on one of the cots, and to her relief, his mother sat next to him. Manuela grabbed an armful of clothes from the floor.

"Sorry." In the dim light, it seemed her cheeks were flushed. "Mama and I try to keep it neat, but it's hard."

"I understand." Six people were living in a room the size of the laundry room at the Flanagan house. No wonder it seemed cluttered. "Let's have a look at Juan."

Nodding to the mother, she bent over the cot. "Hi,

there, Juan. Remember me?" She smiled reassuringly, trying to hide her dismay. His skin was hot and dry, his eyes sunken in his small face. She glanced at Manuela. "Any chance we can get more light in here?"

Nodding, she switched on a battery-powered lantern.

No electricity, overcrowded conditions, inadequate cooking facilities—surely someone like Matthew Dixon could do better than this for his employees, even if they were here for only a short period of time.

She checked the boy's vital signs and cautiously removed the bandage on his head, relieved to find no sign of infection. "It doesn't look as if his injury is causing this, Manuela. Has anyone else been sick?"

Manuela translated quickly for her mother and then nodded. "Some of the other children have had fever and stomach upsets."

"Why didn't their parents bring them to the clinic?"

Manuela shrugged, face impassive. If she knew the answer, she wasn't going to tell.

"Tell your mother I'd like to have Juan checked out by the doctor." She glanced at her watch. "Since it's so late, maybe the best thing is to take him to the E.R."

The mother seemed to understand that phrase. Nodding, she scooped Juan up, wrapping him in a frayed cotton blanket.

Terry followed them out, hoping she was making the right choice. Harriet would come to the camp if she called her, but by the time she'd tracked her down, they could be at the E.R. Jake wasn't on duty tonight, so…

That train of thought sputtered out. Why exactly did she have his schedule down pat in her mind?

Mrs. Ortiz hurried outside. She stopped so suddenly

that Terry nearly bumped into her. Mel Jordan, the crew chief, stood a few feet away, glaring at them.

"Where do you think you're going?" He planted beefy hands on his hips.

Terry stepped around the woman. "Juan is running a fever. We're taking him in to have the doctor look at him."

"You people aren't supposed to be here." He jerked his head toward the building. "Take the kid back inside. You don't want to go running around this time of night."

Mrs. Ortiz started to turn, but Terry caught her arm. Manuela moved to her mother's other side, so that the three of them faced the man.

"My car is at the clinic." She tried to keep her voice pleasant, suppressing the urge to rage at the man. "I'll run them to the hospital and bring them back. It's not necessary for you to come."

His face darkened. "I told you you're not supposed to be here, interfering in what doesn't concern you." He took a step toward her, the movement threatening. "Just get out and take your do-good notions with you. We don't need outsiders around here stirring up trouble."

Her heart thudded, but she wouldn't let him see fear. "You've got trouble already. The child is sick. You can't keep him from medical care. Or any of the other children."

It was obvious why none of the parents had brought their children to the clinic. Mrs. Ortiz trembled. Surely she didn't think the man would dare become violent....

And if he does, what will you do, Terry? Once again you've leaped into a situation without thinking.

Well, she didn't need to think about it to know these people needed help. What kind of a paramedic would she be if she walked away? One way or another, she was getting this child to a physician.

A pair of headlights slashed through the dusk as a car bucketed down the lane. Distracted, the crew chief spun to stare as the car pulled to a stop a few feet away, the beams outlining their figures.

She was caught in the act. She wouldn't have to take Juan to a doctor. Jake had come to him.

Jake took his time turning off the ignition and getting out of the car. He needed the extra minutes to get his anger under control. One day into the program, and Terry had broken his rules already.

She'd also, from the tension in their stances when his headlights had picked them out, put herself in a bad situation. There had been something menacing about the way the crew chief confronted her, moderating Jake's anger with fear for her.

The man—Jordan, he remembered—swung toward him. "What is this? A convention? Don't you people have enough to do without bothering us?"

Jake let his gaze rest on the man until Jordan shifted his weight nervously. Then he turned toward Terry.

Her shoulders tensed, as if expecting an assault. But no matter how tempted he might be, he owed Terry a certain amount of professional courtesy.

"What do we have, Ms. Flanagan?"

Her breath caught a little. "Juan Ortiz, age six. You'll recall he was treated in the E.R. Temp 103, upset stomach, dehydrated. I was about to bring him to the E.R. when Mr. Jordan intervened."

He knew enough about Terry to know she couldn't

turn away from a sick child. His gaze sliced to Jordan. "Why were you trying to keep them from taking the child to the hospital?"

Jordan's face twisted into a conciliatory smile. "Look, it was just a misunderstanding. I'd never do a thing like that."

He felt Terry's rejection of the words as if they were touching. Well, they'd deal with Jordan later. The important thing now was the child.

"Let's go inside and examine Juan. Then we can see what else is necessary."

The girl, Manuela, explained to her mother in a flood of Spanish, and they all trooped into the cement block building that appeared to be home.

A few minutes later he tousled Juan's hair. "You're going to be fine, young man." He glanced at Terry, naming the medications he wanted. "You have all that at the clinic?"

She nodded. "I'll run over and get them."

"Wait. I'll drive you." And we'll talk. He turned back to Manuela. "I'm writing down all the instructions for you. It's very important to give him liquids, but just a little at a time. A couple of sips every ten or fifteen minutes. You'll make sure your mother understands?"

"Yes, doctor." She straightened, as if with pride. "I will take care of Juan myself. Everything will be done exactly as you say."

"Good girl. You sound as if you'd make a good doctor or nurse one day."

He saw something in her face then—an instant of longing, dashed quickly by hopelessness. He'd seen that look before. It shouldn't be found on children's faces.

"I would like, yes. But it's not possible. This is my life." Her gesture seemed to take in the fields, the building, the people.

"But, Manuela—" Terry began.

He shook his head at her and she fell silent. Now was not the time. But her expression made him fear Terry was taking off on another crusade.

"Well, you can practice your skills with your little brother." He handed her the instructions. "Do you understand all that?"

She read through it quickly and nodded.

"Good girl. He'll be a lot more comfortable once we get his fever down. We'll be back in a few minutes with the medication, okay?"

"Okay." Her smile blossomed, seeming to light the drab room.

He glanced at Terry. "Shall we go?"

She picked up her kit. "I'm ready."

They walked to the car in silence. He'd intended to read the riot act to Terry once they were alone, but by the time they were bouncing down the lane, his anger had dissipated.

She was the one to break the silence. "Why did you come?"

He shrugged. "I wanted to check on how the first day went. Instead I found your car there, you gone. This seemed the likely place."

"You mean you expected me to break the rules." She sounded ready for battle.

"Let's say I wasn't entirely surprised."

"The child was sick. What did you expect me to do?"

"You should have called me. Look, Terry, I understand why you went, but that's not acceptable. If it happens again, I'll pull the plug on the clinic."

Her hands clenched into fists on her knees. "You're pretty good at that, aren't you? Cutting your losses."

The jab went right under his defenses, leaving him breathless for an instant. He yanked the wheel, pulling to a stop in front of the clinic. Before she could get out, he grabbed the door handle, preventing her from moving. They were very close in the dark confines of the car.

"I thought we were going to leave the past behind." He grated the words through the pain.

"I'm sorry." It was a bare whisper, and the grief arced between them. "I shouldn't have said anything."

"No. You shouldn't have."

This was no good. They were both trapped by what had happened, and he didn't see that ever changing.

Chapter Four

Terry walked back into the clinic, aware of Jake pacing behind her. Why didn't he just leave and let her take care of getting the meds to Manuela? The last thing she needed was to have him trailing along behind her as if she couldn't be trusted to do a simple thing like this.

And does he know that he can trust you, Theresa? The voice of her conscience sounded remarkably like her mother. *You certainly haven't shown him that you'll follow his rules so far.*

Even worse, she'd brought up the past that both of them knew they'd have to ignore if they were to have any sort of working relationship. She had to do better—had to find a way to curb her tongue, along with that Flanagan temper that flared too easily.

She took a small cooler from the shelf and began filling it with ice.

"The antibiotic doesn't have to be refrigerated."

He was second-guessing her already. She would not reply in kind, but her lip was going to get sore from biting it if she had to be around Jake too much.

"I know. I thought Manuela could give Juan some ice chips to suck on."

He gave a short nod and took the cooler from her, holding it while she scooped the rest of the ice in. "Where is the drug box?" His voice sharpened. "Surely you didn't leave it here with the clinic unattended."

She held back a sarcastic reply with more control than she'd thought she possessed. She met his gaze. "It's locked in the trunk of my car."

"Good." He snapped the word, but then he shook his head. "Sorry. That wasn't an accusation."

She supposed that was an olive branch. A good working relationship, she reminded herself. You don't have to like the man, just get along with him professionally.

"I know. Believe me, being responsible for that drug box is at the top of my list." She hesitated. How much more should she say about what had happened tonight? "My family always accuses me of leaping before I look. I guess I proved them right tonight, didn't I? I reacted on instinct."

That was an apology, if he'd take it that way.

"Fast reactions are important for first responders like paramedics—"

She had a feeling there was a *but* coming at the end of that sentence. "Don't forget I'm a firefighter, too. Sometimes it's tough to keep the jobs sorted out."

He blinked. "I didn't realize that. In the city, being a paramedic is a full-time job."

"It's what I'm doing most of the time, but our department isn't all that big. When an alarm comes, I do whatever I have to." She smiled. "Can't let the rest of the family down."

Now she'd confused him. "The rest of the family?"

"All of the Flanagans are associated with the fire department in one way or another. My father and one of his brothers started the tradition, and our generation just carried it on. Even my cousin, Brendan, the one you met at the board meeting—"

He nodded, frowning a little, as if that board meeting wasn't the happiest of memories.

"Brendan's the pastor of Grace Church, but he's also the fire department chaplain. He manages to put himself in harm's way a little too often to suit his wife. The others—well, you'll meet them all at the picnic on Sunday."

This was the point at which he could make some excuse to get out of Mom's impulsive invitation. He probably wanted to.

"I'll look forward to that." He paused, his arm brushing hers as he reached for the lid of the cooler. "Unless that's going to be uncomfortable for you. If you'd prefer I not come, I'll respect that."

He was too close, and she was too aware of him. Instead of looking up at his face, she focused on his capable fingers, snapping the cooler lid in place as efficiently as he'd stitch a cut.

An armistice between them—that was what she needed. Maybe letting him see the Flanagans in full force would help that along. Besides, as Mom had said, they'd all be on her side, whether she wanted their help or not.

The silence had stretched too long between them. He'd think she was making too much of this.

"Of course I want you to come." She met his gaze, managing a smile. "You're new in town. We all want to make you feel welcome." Even though she'd rather he'd found any hospital in the country other than Suffolk's Providence Hospital to work in.

"I'll look forward to it, then."

"Fine. I'll write up the directions to my brother's farm for you." A truce, she reminded herself.

She began sorting the intake forms that had been left on the desk. "I'll just put these away and then run the meds over to the camp on my way out. If you'd like to leave, please don't feel you have to stay around."

"I'll take the meds over." He shook his head before she could get a protest out. "It's not a reflection on you, Terry. I just think it's safer if you don't go over there tonight. In fact, no one should be at the clinic alone."

"Shall I add that to the rules?" She couldn't keep the sarcasm out of her voice, and his mouth tightened.

"The rules are designed to keep everyone safe. Including you. But you have to follow them."

"I know." *Stop making him angry, you idiot.* "Next time anything comes up, I'll call the hospital first."

"No, call me. You have my cell number, don't you?"

She nodded. "But you weren't on duty tonight. Wouldn't you rather we call the E.R.?" And now she'd let him know that she was keeping tabs on his schedule.

"That doesn't matter. I'd prefer to be called, so I know firsthand what's happening here. The welfare of the patients and the staff are my responsibility."

That almost sounded as if he cared about the clinic, instead of finding it an unwelcome burden foisted on him by the hospital administration.

"I'm glad you feel that way. It's good to know we can count on you."

She glanced at him, but he wasn't looking at her.

Instead he was frowning at the cement block wall, as if he saw something unpleasant written there.

"My responsibility," he repeated. Then he focused on her, the frown deepening. "Look, it's just as well you understand this. Anything that goes wrong at the clinic is going to reflect on me in the long run. And I don't intend to have my position jeopardized by other people's mistakes. Is that clear?"

Crystal clear. She nodded.

It really was a shame. Just when she began to think Jake was actually human, he had to turn around and prove he wasn't.

"Dr. Landsdowne, may I have a word, please?"

The voice of the hospital administrator stopped Jake in his tracks. It felt as if William Morley had been dogging his steps ever since the migrant clinic program got off the ground. He turned, pinning a pleasant look on his face, and stepped out of the way of a linen cart being pushed down the hospital hallway.

"I'm on my way down to the E.R., Mr. Morley. Can it wait until later?"

Morley's smile thinned. "I won't take much of your time, Doctor. Have you read the memorandum I sent you regarding cutting costs in emergency services?"

Every department in any hospital got periodic memos regarding cutting costs from the administrator—it was part of the administrator's job. Morley did seem to be keeping an eagle eye on the E.R., though.

"Yes, I've been giving it all due attention." How did the man expect him to assess cutting costs when he'd only been in the department for a couple of weeks?

Morley frowned. "In that case, I'd expected an answer from you by this time, detailing the ways in which you expect to save the hospital money in your department."

Jake held on to his temper with an effort. He couldn't afford to antagonize the man. "It's important to take the time to do the job right, don't you agree? I'm still assessing the needs and the current staffing."

"Perhaps if that were your first priority, you'd be able to get to it more quickly."

He stiffened. "The first priority of the chief of emergency services is to provide proper care for the patients who come through our doors."

"Well, of course, I understand that." Morley said the words mechanically and leaned a bit closer, as if what he had to say was a secret between the two of them. "However, the hospital has to make cuts if it's going to remain solvent. We can't afford to have money bleeding out of the E.R. every month. We need an E.R. chief who can make it run efficiently. I hope that's you."

Money wasn't the only thing bleeding in the E.R., but it seemed unlikely Morley was ever going to understand that. The threat was clear enough, though.

"I'll work on it. Now, if you'll excuse me—"

Morley caught his arm. "Another thing—I'm sure you're spending more time than you'd like dealing with this migrant clinic."

Jake nodded. The need to approve every step taken by trained nurses and paramedics was tedious, but he couldn't see any other way of dealing with the situation.

"It occurs to me that something might come up— perhaps has already come up—that the board would find a logical reason to postpone this effort until another time."

The man was obviously fishing for any excuse to shut down the clinic. Jake's mind flashed to the incident two nights earlier when Terry had gone to the migrant housing, clearly breaking his rules. If he told Morley about it, the daily hassle of supervising the clinic might be over.

But he couldn't do it, no matter how much the clinic worried him. He'd promised Terry another chance. His mind presented him with an image of Terry's face, stricken and pale when he'd lit into her team, accusing them of negligence in failing to save Meredith.

No. He owed her something for that.

The wail of a siren was a welcome interruption. He gave Morley a perfunctory smile. "There haven't been any problems there yet. Now, if you'll excuse me, I'm on duty."

This time he escaped, pushing through the swinging door into the E.R.

The paramedics wheeled the patient in just as he arrived. Terry and her partner. He'd just been thinking of her, and here she was.

Terry gave him a cool nod as her partner reeled off the vital statistics—an elderly woman complaining of chest pain and difficulty breathing. He focused on the patient, who looked remarkably composed for someone brought in by paramedics.

He nodded to the nurse. "We'll take it from here."

Terry patted the elderly woman. "You listen to the doc now, Mrs. Jefferson. Everything will be fine."

"Thank you, dear. I don't know what I'd do if I couldn't count on you." The woman beamed at the paramedics.

He flashed a glance at Terry, who was fanning her flushed face. Her red curls were damp with perspiration and her neat navy shirt was wrinkled. "Stick around for a few minutes. I'd like to speak to you."

She nodded, and he helped push the stretcher back to an exam room.

It didn't take more than a few minutes to determine what he'd already suspected—there was nothing wrong with the woman that merited a trip to the emergency room. The fact that the nurse also knew Mrs. Jefferson well enough to know she'd like grape juice just confirmed it. He left the woman happily drinking her grape juice and went in search of the paramedics team.

He caught up with Terry in the hallway. "Where's your partner?"

She swung toward him, resting a frosty water bottle against her temple. "Jeff's restocking the unit. Do you want me to get him?"

"Not necessary. I can say what I need to say to you." And he shouldn't be noticing how those damp red curls clung to her skin. Terry didn't mean anything to him except an obstacle to be overcome. "That woman shouldn't have been brought to the E.R. There's nothing wrong with her."

"That decision isn't really up to the paramedics, is it? We don't practice medicine."

He glanced around, but no one was in earshot. "Are you throwing my words back at me?"

Terry's face crinkled into a sudden smile. "Sorry. It's just that we all know Mrs. Jefferson is a frequent flyer."

"Frequent flyer?" He understood, all right, although he hadn't heard them called that—those people who called the paramedics when they got lonely or needed attention.

"Look, she lives alone in a third-floor walk-up and

her air conditioner just broke. I suppose she got a little scared. Anybody might in this heat. It happens."

"I know it happens, but it shouldn't." This was exactly the sort of thing Morley had been talking about. "It wastes the hospital's resources."

Terry looked unimpressed. "I don't work for the hospital, I work for the city."

He planted his hands on his hips. It was probably a good thing, for Terry's sake, that she didn't work for the hospital.

"That's not the point. We have to cut costs in the E.R., and every patient that's brought in here for no reason eats into our budget."

"She probably doesn't need a thing except to rest in a cool place for a while. That's not going to take any of your budget."

"She can find a cool place in a movie theater." He stopped short, realizing he was letting himself get into an argument with a paramedic. "Take her home. Now."

Terry looked at him as if she could hardly believe her ears. "You can't expect us to haul her back to that hot apartment now. Give me a few hours. I'll call Brendan and see if he can't get someone to donate a new air conditioner."

Brendan Flanagan, her minister cousin. The board member. Being caught between a board member and the hospital administrator was not a good place to be. For a moment longer he glared at Terry, annoyed at her ability to put him on the spot.

But this was a no-win situation. "All right. But she's not staying for supper. You and your partner get back here for her before five, or I'll call her a cab."

"Right. We'll do that." She spun, obviously not eager to spend any more time in his company.

He stood for a moment, watching the trim, uniformed figure making for the door. At the last moment she stopped, turned and pulled something from her pocket.

She came back to him and held out a folded slip of paper. "I nearly forgot to give you this." She stuffed it in his hand and hurried out the door.

Jake unfolded the paper. It was a carefully drawn map, designed to take him to the Flanagan picnic on Sunday.

He didn't suppose he could get out of that picnic without offending several people, including one who was on the hospital board. But he suspected that, if Terry had anything to say about it, he wasn't going to enjoy himself.

The hot day had given way to a sticky, humid evening, with clouds thickening. A shower would be nice, Terry thought hopefully as she slid out of the car. But if they did get one this time of year, it would be a thunderstorm. She walked toward the back door of the comfortable house that had sheltered three generations of Flanagans.

Mom was in the kitchen, wiping cookie dough off the table. The aroma of chocolate chip cookies filled the air, and red geraniums rioted on the windowsills. She looked up, smiling as always. Mom always made you feel as if you were the best thing she'd seen all day.

Terry put one arm around her mother's waist while snagging a handful of still-warm cookies with the other hand.

Mom kissed her cheek and gave a laughing swipe at her hand. "Someday you're not going to be able to eat like that, Terry."

"Then I'd better take advantage of it while I can. Umm." She slid onto the stool next to the pine table. "Which of your grandchildren do I have to thank for the cookie baking today?"

"Mary Kate dropped the children off while she did some shopping. She's insisting she has to look for a job, and she needs some interview clothes that make her look like a physical therapist instead of a mom."

Terry sank down on the kitchen stool. "That wasn't the life she and Kenny had planned. They always felt it so important that she stay home with the children."

"Life changes when we least expect it." Her mother took a package of chicken from the refrigerator and opened it. "Losing Kenny hit Mary Kate hard. She hasn't discovered all her strength yet."

Terry blinked. "What do you mean? She always seems to keep her feelings under control."

"I'm not sure what I mean." The admission was unusual for Mom, who'd always seemed the source of all answers to Terry. "At first I thought she was coping well with Kenny's death. Now, I'm not so sure. She's hiding something behind that cheerful face she puts on."

"Have you tried to' talk to her?" That was a silly question. Of course Mom would have tried.

Mom's hand slowed on the piece of chicken she was breading, as if she'd forgotten what she was doing. "She's not willing to let me in. Maybe you ought to talk to her."

"Me?" Terry nearly choked on her cookie. "Mary Kate treats me like I'm about eleven. She'd never confide in me. And I doubt that I could give her any good advice, especially since…"

"Since what?"

She shrugged, evading those wise eyes. "You know. Having Jake Landsdowne around hasn't exactly done great things for my self-confidence."

"Terry, you know perfectly well that you're very good at what you do. You shouldn't let that man's opinion matter so much to you."

"I know, I know. But he's in charge—at least of the migrant clinic." She stood, shrugging. "Well, no point in talking about it. I'll set the table. Is it just the three of us tonight?"

"Just us."

Time was, they'd been hard put to fit the whole family around the dining room table. With her three brothers and cousin Brendan married now, supper was a much quieter affair most of the time, although people still seemed to show up at suppertime with the flimsiest of excuses.

She carried service for three through the swinging door into the dining room and began laying the table automatically.

Her mother didn't understand. Terry had been confident of her abilities before, when she'd gone off to Philadelphia to try her wings on her own, without the support of her big, loving, interfering family. That confidence had been shattered into a million pieces by what happened when Meredith Stanley died, and since then she'd struggled to put it back together, one patient at a time.

Now Jake was here, and she had to see him nearly every time she went to the E.R., had to cope with his criticisms of the way she was running the clinic, too. Small wonder she kept second-guessing herself.

Her mother pushed through the swinging door, a

bowl of tossed salad in her hands. She set it down and gave Terry a searching look. "What is it? I can see something else has happened."

"I never could keep secrets from you, could I?" She managed a smile.

Her mother clasped her hand warmly. "You have a warm, open, loving spirit. That's not a bad thing, although maybe it opens you up to hurt sometimes. Now tell me."

"It's not a big deal, I guess. We had a call from Mrs. Jefferson today." She didn't need to identify the woman further. Her mother had heard about all their regulars. "Her air conditioner had broken, and she was sweltering in that walk-up apartment."

"Poor thing. What did you do about it?" Of course Mom understood she'd had to do something.

"We took her in to the E.R. And I called Brendan. He managed to get an air conditioner from somebody, and he was over there installing it by the time we took her home."

"What was the problem, then?"

"Jake. Dr. Landsdowne. He knew there wasn't anything wrong with her, and he wanted us to take her straight back home. Said the E.R. couldn't afford to have people there who didn't need the care."

Her mother gave her a shrewd look. "I take it you had words about it."

"We did." She shook her head. "I keep trying to get along with him—honestly I do. I've prayed and prayed about it." Although if truth be told, mostly she was praying not to run into him. "Anyway, he finally agreed to let her stay for the afternoon. You'd have thought I was asking him to give her free plastic surgery for the rest of her life."

"Now, Terry, I'm sure he wasn't that bad. I heard about his service in Somalia. Surely that means his heart is in the right place."

"I guess so. But he's doing a good job of hiding it from me."

"Then maybe that's what we'd better take to the Lord." She took both Terry's hands in hers. "All right?"

Terry nodded. Mom had always taught them that they could pray anytime, anyplace, and the more often, the better.

"Lord, we want to bring this situation with Dr. Landsdowne to you." Mom sounded so warm when she prayed, as if she were having an intimate conversation with a dear friend who already knew all her troubles. "We know he and Terry can find a way to get along, if only he'll show us the spirit that took him to do Your work in such a difficult place. Please open his heart, and open ours to see who he really is. In Jesus's precious name. Amen."

Mom's warmth and faith surrounded her, and some of the tightness she'd been holding on to slipped away. Mom's prayer hadn't quite been what she'd have prayed, though. She wasn't so sure she wanted to know Jake any better than she already did.

Chapter Five

"Hey, Aunt Terry, play football with us!" Terry's niece Shawna punctuated the request by flinging the foam football straight at her. Terry grabbed it instinctively, nearly falling out of the lawn chair she'd positioned under the oak tree that shaded the yard at Gabe and Nolie's farm.

"C'mon, Shawna, it's too hot for football." In fact, lounging in a lawn chair watching the rest of the Flanagan clan scurry around getting the weekly picnic together sounded just right, if a little lazy.

Shawna, Mary Kate's eight-year-old, was the ring-leader of the Flanagan grandchildren. She gathered the others around her, blue eyes sparkling, dimples flashing, and Terry knew her moments in the lawn chair were going to be short-lived.

A moment later, the chair collapsed under the rush of small bodies, leaving Terry laughing helplessly, tickling or kissing any niece or nephew she could reach.

"Is that your idea of helping?" Seth, her second-oldest

brother, reached into the tangle of bodies and pulled out Davy, his son, giving him a kiss before setting him on his feet. "Getting the kids so riled up they won't want to eat?"

"Hey, I'm going to help them work up an appetite." She scrambled up, tossing the football in the air. "You want to help?"

Seth gave her the quick grin that had always made him everyone's buddy. "Thanks anyway. I promised to help Gabe get the ice-cream maker ready."

Even his promotion to captain in the fire department hadn't changed Seth's easygoing, steady outlook. In fact, since he'd married Julie, providing himself and Davy with the person they needed to make their family complete, she'd seldom seen him without a smile on his face.

She faked a punch at his midsection. "Looks like married life agrees with you. Next thing you know, you'll be growing a paunch."

"No chance." He patted his flat stomach. "Davy keeps me hopping, and when the new baby comes, I'll probably be walking the floor at night."

He glanced toward the picnic table, where Julie was helping Mom spread the tablecloth. The soft yellow top Julie wore accentuated her rounded belly.

The blaze of fierce love in his face startled Terry. Maybe Seth wasn't so calm and collected as all that, at least where his love was concerned.

He ruffled her curls, something her brothers had been doing to emphasize their height for years. "When are you going to take the plunge? Hasn't Mom rounded up any likely prospects for you yet?"

"Mom knows better."

"What about this new doc who's coming to dinner today? Julie and I thought maybe—"

"No chance." She couldn't say the words fast enough. Mom wouldn't have told anyone but Dad about her history with Jake, so maybe it was natural that they'd jump to that conclusion. "He's just one of Mom's good deeds. I think she's hoping it will make him a little easier to get along with at the migrant clinic. He's been driving us crazy with all his rules."

Seth put his arm around her shoulders. "Want us to throw a scare into him? The Flanagan boys can still look pretty fierce if we want to."

"Like you used to scare off all my boyfriends? No, thanks." She ducked away from him, hoping he was deceived by her light tone. "If you want to know why I'm still single, just blame it on yourself. Go get the ice cream ready. And shout when you need someone to turn the handle. All the kids want a chance."

Laughing, Seth walked toward the farmhouse. Terry tossed the football to Mandy, Ryan's little stepdaughter. She couldn't look at Mandy now, laughing and chattering a mile a minute, without remembering the first time she'd seen her, when Ryan had carried her out of a burning building. Mandy was one of God's small miracles, now a part of their lives to stay.

She'd been kidding when she'd told Seth he'd scared off all her boyfriends, but there was an element of truth in that. Much as she loved her brothers, they could be a bit overwhelming. Any boy would have been wary of running afoul of Gabe, or Seth, or Ryan, or even Brendan, the cousin who'd been raised as one of them.

Not that she thought they'd try to scare Jake. Or that

he'd scare if they did. But they'd always been so protective of Terry, their baby sister. She'd always known she had them to fall back on.

That should be a good thing, shouldn't it? But on the one occasion when she'd left Suffolk to try life on her own in the big city, she'd failed.

Terry calmed an argument between Shawna and Michael, her little brother, and sent Michael running toward the paddock for a long pass. The donkey lifted his head, watching the small figure running toward him. Toby was used to their shenanigans by this time.

She didn't want to think about that time in Philadelphia, because every time she did, it brought her right back to Jake. She glanced at her watch. He was late. Was it too much to hope that he wasn't coming?

Michael hurtled back to her, his face red.

"Listen, guys, I think we'd better stop and have a nice cold drink, okay? It's getting too hot to run around."

A chorus of groans greeted her, but she shepherded them toward the table, where a thermos of lemonade and another of iced tea sat waiting, and supervised the process of pouring lemonade into paper cups.

"Let's play another game, Aunt Terry, please?" Shawna leaned against her, wheedling. "It doesn't have to be a running game."

Terry dropped a kiss on Shawna's red curls. "I have a better idea. See Grandpa sitting there relaxing? Go ask him to tell you a story."

"Yeah, a story." Michael ran toward Dad, lemonade sloshing in his cup, and the others followed.

Dad gave them a mock fierce frown as they interrupted his discussion with Brendan of his favorite football team's chances, but she wasn't fooled. There was nothing Dad liked better than a fresh audience of little kids for his stories. Only Gabe and Nolie's one-year-old, asleep on a blanket in the shade, was still too young to understand Grandpa's tales.

Nolie, Gabe's wife, set a bowl of potato salad on the table. "We were going to start bringing the food out, but I guess your friend from the hospital isn't here yet. Should we wait awhile?"

"No, let's go ahead. Maybe he'll be here by the time it's ready." And maybe he wouldn't be.

She ought to be ashamed of herself. During worship that morning, she'd achieved a sense of peace, asking God to use her in this situation for His good ends. Now, it seemed, she was already frittering away those good intentions by hoping Jake wouldn't show up at all. She closed her eyes for a quick prayer.

I'm sorry, Father. I mean well, You know that. I just keep getting in the way of my own prayers. Please help me to deal with Jake the way You want me to, and guide my words and my thoughts when I'm with him.

Gravel churned under car wheels. She opened her eyes. Jake's car came up the farm lane and pulled to a stop along a row of lilac bushes. Her stomach gave a little jolt. God was giving her an immediate opportunity to test her resolve.

Jake cut the engine and sat motionless for a moment. He'd thought seriously about calling Mrs. Flanagan with an excuse, but decided that would be the coward's way out. Any excuse he'd made would simply look as if he didn't want to encounter Terry again after the clashes they'd had recently.

He couldn't do that. He might wish Terry were a bit more amenable to direction, but she was a good paramedic, and she was certainly devoted to her patients. That was the bottom line—patient care. That was something Morley, the hospital administrator, didn't seem to understand.

More to the point, he couldn't afford to antagonize a board member like Brendan Flanagan. His position was precarious enough already without doing that. So he'd go through with this, and he'd make a good impression on the Flanagan family if it killed him.

He got out and started toward the farmhouse. This didn't look like any working farm that he'd ever seen, not that he knew much about it. From the lane, green lawn stretched toward a white frame farmhouse with a wide, welcoming porch. Beyond was a garage whose double doors stood open, exposing what looked like some kind of obstacle course.

There was a cottage, like a smaller replica of the main house, its front door flanked with rosebushes, and a red barn whose white-fenced paddock held a few animals he couldn't identify from this distance.

But it was the lawn that drew his attention. The scene was like a Flemish painting—people dotted across the grass, adults and children both, rustic wooden tables spread with white cloths for a picnic. Surely all those people weren't Flanagans. He'd expected a quiet family meal with maybe eight or ten people at the most. There were at least twice that many, it seemed, and they were all staring at him.

He hadn't felt this awkward since he'd started a new school in the eighth grade. Well, that was stupid. His confidence wasn't so badly damaged—he could still meet a bunch of strangers and make a good impression.

Terry detached herself from the group and came toward him. In jeans and a bright yellow T-shirt, she looked younger than she did in uniform. She moved reluctantly, he suspected. He could hardly blame her. Things between them had been difficult, to say the least. She'd probably have rescinded her mother's impulsive invitation if she could.

"Welcome to Nolie's Ark." If her smile was forced, it didn't show. "Did you have any trouble finding the place?"

"Not at all. The map brought me directly here." He'd noticed the unusual sign, with its fanciful ark loaded with all sorts of animals. "Why Nolie's Ark?"

Terry's dimples flashed. "Wait until we've shown you around. Then you'll understand. And Nolie's because the farm belonged to my sister-in-law before she and Gabe married. He wouldn't let her change the name."

"Gabe is your brother?" He had a feeling keeping everyone straight would be a job.

"The oldest. Come and meet everyone."

He fell into step with her. "I thought this was just going to be family today. I didn't expect such a crowd."

Terry's grin widened. "It is family. Sorry, I guess someone should have warned you about the size of the Flanagan clan. I'm afraid we can be a little overwhelming at first."

"Just at first?"

She chuckled. "You might have a point."

They'd reached the table. Apparently aware that

they'd been staring at him, people began talking to each other again. He was just as happy not to be the center of attention.

Terry led him to the man at the grill loaded with sizzling hot dogs and hamburgers. "This is my brother, Gabe."

"Your big brother," Gabe corrected, extending his hand. "Welcome to our home."

Tall, with dark hair and blue eyes, Gabe didn't look much like Terry, but Jake saw a strong resemblance to Mrs. Flanagan. A handsome yellow Labrador retriever sat at Gabe's side.

"Thanks for inviting me. I appreciate the chance to get to know a few people." And possibly mend a few fences with a board member while I'm at it. He'd already spotted Brendan at the end of the table, bouncing a toddler on his lap.

"That's my wife, Nolie." Gabe nodded toward a slender blonde in a denim skirt and blue shirt, who was lifting the lid from a large casserole dish. "They've just put the food on, so why don't you find a seat. Terry can introduce you around while we're eating." He grinned, and now Jake saw the resemblance to Terry. "That might be easier than trying to remember a whole string of names."

Nolie clinked a glass, and the chatter slowly died out. He slid onto the end of a bench next to Terry as Pastor Brendan folded his hands. Heads bowed around the table.

"Father, You've given us another beautiful day to share Your bounty together, and we ask Your blessing and care for those who aren't as fortunate as we are. We thank You for this food and the hands that prepared it. We ask Your blessings on this family and on the new friend You've brought into our midst today. In Jesus's name. Amen."

A chorus of amens sounded around the table. One of a pair of small redheads tugged at Brendan's sleeve. "You didn't say God bless the animals, Uncle Brendan."

"You're right, Michael, I didn't." He bowed his head again. "And bless the animals, too. Amen." He grinned. "Let's eat."

Serving dishes began to fly around the table at what seemed the speed of light. Mrs. Flanagan, across from him, snatched a bowl of potato salad from her oldest son and offered it to Jake.

"Please, have some." She gave him the sweet smile that had lured him into this family meal. "You have to fend for yourself around here or you won't get a thing."

"Now, Mom, we're a little more polite than that." Terry passed a crock of baked lima beans. "The speed just comes of having eight people around the table when we were growing up, four of them growing boys."

"Eight?" he echoed faintly as an airborne biscuit was snatched midair by Pastor Brendan, of all people.

Terry nodded, passing a bowl of coleslaw. "My sister Mary Kate is the oldest." She nodded to a slightly older version of herself, leaning across to fork chicken onto the plate of one of the children. "The two little redheads are hers—Shawna and Michael."

"Which one is her husband?"

Terry's face went somber. "Kenny died nine months ago. Liver cancer. Things went so fast I'm not sure she's accepted it, even now."

"That's rough." He caught the wave of sorrow she felt for her sister, a little startled that he responded to her emotions so quickly.

"Yes. It is." Her gaze was fixed on the roll she was but-tering. "Gabe comes next—that's his and Nolie's toddler, Siobhan, sitting on Brendan's lap. They run this place."

"As a farm?" he ventured.

She smiled. "Not quite. Nolie trains service animals and then works with disabled individuals to bring them together with the right animals. That's how Gabe and Nolie met."

He glanced toward the dog, lying quietly behind Gabe, brown eyes watchful. "You mean the dog—"

"Max is a seizure alert dog. Gabe's a firefighter, injured in the line of duty. Now he helps Nolie with the animals and teaches at the fire academy."

"Dr. Landsdowne, glad to meet you." The bluff, hearty man who sat next to Siobhan Flanagan must be Terry's father. Clearly, that was where she'd gotten the red hair and freckles, although her father's hair was turning white. "I'm Joe Flanagan. Theresa's falling down on the introductions."

Jake reached across to shake hands. "A pleasure to meet you, sir."

"I'm just trying to introduce Jake slowly—" Terry stopped, flushing. "I mean, Dr. Landsdowne."

"I think it better be Jake when we're not on the job, don't you?" he said easily.

"Jake." Joe's handshake was firm. "Terry, the man's a doctor. I'm sure he can keep a few names straight." He nodded toward the other side of the long table. "That's Seth, our next son, with his wife, Julie. Little Davy belongs to them. And you know Brendan."

"I met him through the hospital board. Isn't he Terry's cousin?"

"My brother's boy. We raised him after his parents

died. His wife, Claire, is an old friend of Nolie's. Then comes Theresa, and Ryan is the youngest, though he and Terry are so close in age they've always been like twins. That's him, with his wife, Laura, and their daughter, Mandy."

The names swam around in his mind. Maybe Terry's method would have been better. He turned toward her, but Gabe's little girl had toddled over to her, and she scooped the baby up in her arms.

"This is little Siobhan." She nuzzled the soft blond curls on the baby's neck. "She's our latest addition. Isn't she beautiful?"

She smiled at him, face glowing with love for her tiny niece. It was like leaning near a warm fire on a cold night, and the urge to draw closer surprised and cautioned him with its strength.

"Beautiful," he agreed. Joe had turned away to talk to someone else. "You really are all following your father's footsteps. I suppose he expected that."

"Oh, I guess he'd have been proud of us, no matter what we wanted to do. It just runs in the family."

The way being a doctor ran in his family, but it wasn't as if he and his sister had had a choice. The Flanagan kids apparently felt they did, but chose it anyway.

Otherwise, the Flanagan crew was as different from his family as it was possible to be. He couldn't imagine this babble of cheerful noise at any Landsdowne family gathering, and his sister's children would be tidied away long before the adults sat down at a linen-covered table for a meal prepared by the cook and a little civil conversation.

"Do you do this sort of thing often? Get together

with the whole family, I mean." He gestured at the crowded table.

"Every Sunday," Terry said. Her eyes narrowed. "I suppose that sounds odd to you."

"Well, it—" It did sound odd, at least in his experience, for grown children to be so close to their parents, but he could hardly say so. "You seem to depend on each other a great deal."

"What's wrong with that?" The snap in Terry's voice told him she'd taken offense. "We're a family. Naturally we stick together. Or don't you think that's natural?"

Why on earth did she have to take offense at everything he said? He'd come here to mend fences, not start a war. "I didn't mean—" he began calmly, but Mrs. Flanagan stood up and caught Terry's hand.

"Terry, come along and help me with the dessert. You can finish your conversation later." She practically dragged Terry away from the table.

Wise woman. She'd seen trouble coming and headed it off, but he'd still somehow have to convince Terry that he hadn't been criticizing. She seemed constantly ready to think the worst of him. Of course, she'd say she had good reason for that.

"Keep you hand flat, Mandy." Terry put a carrot on her small niece's palm. "You don't want Toby to think your fingers are carrots, do you?"

Mandy giggled, stretching her arm through the paddock rails toward the gray donkey. Toby, used to children, waited patiently until her hand uncurled, and then delicately took the carrot.

"It tickles," Mandy declared. "I love Toby, Aunt Terry."

"I love Toby, too." She gave Mandy a quick squeeze.

"Who is Toby?" The voice came from behind her. "Your boyfriend?"

Mandy and Michael both started to giggle, giving her time to tamp down her irritation and plant a smile on her face before she turned toward Jake. Really, couldn't the man see that she didn't especially want to spend her day off with him?

"Toby's the donkey," Michael explained, recovering first. "Aunt Terry doesn't have a boyfriend. She's a paramedic."

"I don't think the two are mutually exclusive, are they?"

"Michael thinks so." She ruffled Michael's curls, as red as her own. "He's almost seven, so he knows all about it."

Jake leaned over the fence to pat the donkey, listening to the children prattle on about how smart and how sweet he was, and giving her time to catch her breath. Had she overreacted to Jake's comment about the family? Possibly, but she was rather sensitive to the topic of being dependent on her family. He'd hit a sore point without even knowing it.

And probably he'd meant the comment to be just as condescending as she'd taken it. She didn't know what a family like the Landsdownes did together—sat around and talked about complicated surgical procedures, maybe. They probably didn't feed carrots to donkeys, as Jake was doing right now under Mandy's careful tutelage.

"Keep your hand flat," Mandy cautioned, parroting Terry's words to her as she straightened out his long, gifted fingers with her small hand. "You don't want Toby to think your finger is a carrot."

"Certainly not," he agreed. He tilted his head, smiling at Terry as the donkey nibbled the carrot.

She could only hope her face didn't express what she was feeling. She was so accustomed to a frown when Jake looked at her that the easy, relaxed smile knocked her back on her heels. The man had charm when he bothered to use it, which wasn't very often, at least with her.

"Hey, Michael and Mandy!" Gabe shouted from the porch. "Come quick if you want a turn with the ice cream."

The two bolted for the porch, not bothering to say a word.

Jake dusted off his hands. "Guess we know where we stand in the scheme of things. Somewhere below ice cream."

"They love to turn the crank." And they'd left her where she didn't want to be, alone with Jake. "Shall we go and join them?"

She took a step, but he stopped her with a hand on her arm.

"Your mother said you'd show me around," he said. "Why don't we start with the barn?"

That made it impossible for her to refuse, and he knew it. "It's just a barn," she tried feebly.

"I'm a city boy. Humor me."

She managed a smile that was probably more of a grimace and started toward the barn. Well, if he wanted a tour, she'd give him one.

"Nolie says the barn was built in the early eighteen hundreds, and not much has been done to it since then except for basic repair. The style is typical of Pennsylvania German barns. You'll see them all over the county. People know about the Amish in this area, but plenty of the other early settlers were German, too."

"I take it they built to last." He actually sounded interested.

"Seems that way. You really ought to talk to Nolie about it. She's the expert. Her family came over from Germany on William Penn's heels, from the sound of it."

She pushed the heavy door open. Gabe had probably closed it to keep the little ones out. She stepped inside, eyes adjusting gradually to the dim light. The lofty interior was cool after the bright sunshine outside.

"Just a barn," she said, swinging her hand in a gesture meant to take in the stalls, the loft, the stacked hay bales, even the ginger barn cat that leaped softly from a manger, as if to ask what they were doing there.

Jake brushed past her, approaching the chestnut quarter horse that stood in the closest stall. "Why isn't this handsome fellow out in the paddock today?"

She moved reluctantly to join him, and Eagle came over to have his face scratched. "Tact on Nolie's part, I imagine. If Eagle were out where the kids could see him, they'd want to ride him, and most of them are too small. She's just started giving lessons to Shawna, and she probably doesn't want to start a fight over who's big enough."

"Tactful," he agreed, patting Eagle's shining neck. "Now suppose *you* stop being tactful and tell me why you're upset with me."

That startled her into looking up at him. His face was grave and attentive, as if he really cared how she felt.

That was certainly unlikely. He'd never shown much consideration for her feelings before.

"If you must know, I didn't like being made to feel

as if my family were somehow odd because we like to spend time together. I'm sure it's more fashionable to dismiss your parents as irrelevant, but we happen to appreciate ours."

His hand stilled on the horse's neck. "You're right."

"You mean you *were* being condescending."

His lips tightened. "Stop putting words in my mouth, Terry. No, I mean you're right to appreciate your parents. If I had parents like yours, I hope I'd feel the same way."

"Oh." He'd taken the wind out of her sails. "Well, I didn't expect—"

"You didn't expect anything but the worst from me." He swung to face her, close against the rough wood of the stall. "I know we've had our differences, but I thought we'd agreed to put that behind us. Still, you constantly put the worst interpretation on everything I say. Like the situation with your frequent flyer the other day."

Well, she was on solid ground there, whether he agreed or not. "We had to bring her to the E.R. It's not like she did any harm by being there, whether she needed medical care or not."

"Maybe so, but I'd just endured a lecture from the hospital administrator on cutting costs. If he has his way, the E.R. budget will be cut, and someone who really needs care could be turned away."

"Morley." The man's penny-pinching was notorious. "I'm sorry, but what else could I have done? I couldn't walk away and leave her in that stifling apartment." Surely he could see that.

"No. I guess you couldn't." He was looking at her so intently that she felt as if she were under a microscope. "You have a warm heart, and after meeting your family, I understand it." He put his hand over hers on the stall bar, and she seemed to feel his touch shimmering across her skin.

"There's—" Her breath got tangled up, and she had to start again. "There's nothing wrong with having a warm heart, is there?"

"Not a thing. Not a single thing."

He was so close that his breath touched her cheek, so close that she could see the tiny dust motes flickering in the shaft of sunlight that surrounded them. Eagle moved slightly in his stall, his hoofbeat muffled against the straw.

Jake leaned closer, and for an insane moment she thought he was going to kiss her. Then a shout from Gabe startled them and they pulled apart.

"Terry, Jake, the ice cream is ready. You better come before it's all gone."

"Be right there," she called back. She swung toward the door. "We'd better go. They'll eat it in no time flat."

She would not look back at Jake. She wouldn't wonder if he was annoyed at her brother's bad timing.

Maybe it wasn't bad timing at all. Maybe Gabe's interruption had been right on target to keep her from making a fool of herself.

Chapter Six

Jake took the bowl Gabe handed him automatically and stared at creamy vanilla ice cream studded with chunks of peaches. What had just happened to him, aside from the fact that these people expected him to eat a bowlful of cholesterol and calories?

He'd let his guard down far too much with Terry, practically coming right out and saying that he envied her for the family life she'd been blessed with. The opposite, obviously, was that he hadn't.

He put a spoonful in his mouth, and the rich flavor exploded on his tongue. Not good for him, of course, but very good to the taste. Like Terry.

The children were jumping up and down next to him, demanding seconds from the metal ice-cream bucket, nestled in its tub of ice. He took a few steps away from the melee, moving deeper into the shade of the huge oak tree.

Terry wouldn't understand his attitude toward his family. How could she? She only knew what everyone at Philadelphia General had known—just what people had always thought about Jacob Landsdowne III.

Born with a silver spoon in his mouth. The golden boy who had everything going for him, ready to step right into his father's prestigious practice. The guy who really had it made, not like the poor jerks who had to fight every step up the medical ladder and still ended up with a crushing load of debt they'd probably never be able to pay off.

The thing was, those people had never known what the payback was for everything he'd been given—the equally crushing load of obligation, the necessity of being perfect. He didn't want them to know. After all, he had a little pride left.

Across the lawn, Joe Flanagan was laughing, clapping Seth on the back over something. One of the children ran to him, and he caught her up and tossed her into the air, catching her in a bear hug.

No, with a father like hers, Terry wouldn't understand. She probably wouldn't believe that a father could turn his back on his only son for the sin of being imperfect.

Well, enough self-pity. He'd wallowed in that long enough during those weeks in the hospital when he'd come back from Africa. He was finished with that.

This job was his last chance to reestablish himself as a doctor, and he couldn't let anything stand in his way. He had to succeed. And success meant not only proving himself as a doctor but also performing that delicate balancing act between good medicine and hospital profits, between Morley and his balanced books and Pastor Brendan and his good works.

So this picnic wasn't about the excellent food and certainly not about moments alone with Terry. He backed quickly away from the memory of standing so close to her in the barn, sunlight tangling in her red curls, her face tilted up to his.

Last chance. The words echoed in his mind. He had to focus on his goal, eliminating every distraction, especially ones with red hair and a stubborn streak a mile wide.

Pastor Brendan sat at the table, alone for the moment. Carrying the ice cream, he walked over and sat down across from him. "Not indulging in ice cream today, Pastor?"

"Brendan, remember?" Brendan patted his stomach. "I already had a serving of my wife's chocolate soufflé, and I'm stuffed. Claire is teaching herself to cook by working her way through a French cookbook."

"Lucky man."

"I am that." Brendan smiled, his gaze moving to the slim, dark-haired woman who was helping to clear the table. His gaze lingered there for a moment and then came back to Jake. "So, tell me how the clinic is working out. Are you managing to juggle that with your other responsibilities?"

"I've decided to give up sleeping." At the other man's look of concern, he shook his head, forcing an amused expression to his face. "No, just kidding. Terry has her volunteers so well organized that things are running very smoothly."

Except for such problems as Terry's unauthorized visit to the migrant housing, but he didn't think he'd mention that. If she hadn't told her family, he wasn't going to.

"I'm not surprised." Brendan glanced at Terry, who

was pushing a small nephew on the swing tied to one of the oak's branches while she carried on a conversation with Seth's wife. "Terry's always been superb at running her various crusades."

"You mean she does this all the time?" It sounded as if Brendan could give him some valuable insight into what made Terry tick.

"From the time she was a kid, Terry's always been a crusader." He smiled, shaking his head a little. "Oh, maybe some of them were tilting at windmills, but her heart was always in the right place. It still is."

"Yes," he said softly, watching her without intending to. Terry's laugh looked as lighthearted as that of her nephew. "I can see that."

"She used to drag us into her battles, willing or not. Save the whales, save the park, provide Thanksgiving dinner for the hungry…whatever it was, Terry gave it her all."

"I guess the fact that she became a paramedic was a foregone conclusion, then. She wants to save people."

Brendan nodded. "Don't get me wrong, she was a good firefighter, still is. But she's never been content with just putting a fire out. She wants to fix things for people."

"Sort of like her cousin Brendan, then," he said.

Brendan chuckled. "Maybe you have a point there. My church was moving in the direction of helping the migrants already, but Terry just pushed us a little faster. And once I saw what those people are dealing with—" He nodded toward Mary Kate's little redheads, chasing each other around the table with apparently boundless energy. "I'm thankful our little ones don't have to live like that, so that obligates me to help."

"I take it you know Matthew Dixon pretty well, since he attends your church."

"Attends? Not very often. But the Dixons have belonged to Grace Church since it was founded."

Jake chose his words carefully. "I'm concerned that we not start any problems with him through the clinic. He seemed rather short-tempered on the subject the one time I saw him."

"I don't think you have to worry much about that. At least not about Matthew coming around looking for problems. He hasn't been well for the past year or so, and Andrew's really the one who's handling everything."

"Poor old fellow." Siobhan slid onto the bench next to him, abruptly joining the conversation. "He knows he's slipping. It must be terrible to feel you have to depend on your children that much."

"Don't worry, Mom." Terry came up behind her and slung her arm around her mother's shoulders in a quick hug. "When you start losing it, I'll still be there to help."

"Not if I get there first," Brendan said, smiling at his aunt.

Siobhan waved her hand as if waving them off. "The one I keep thinking about is that young girl, Manuela. She seems so bright and hardworking. It's a shame she can't even consider a career in medicine."

So Terry had told her family about Manuela's dreams. He watched her as she slid onto the bench next to him. Did that mean she'd also told them about her unauthorized visit?

Brendan nodded, glancing at the children who were gathering on a blanket in the shade, apparently to listen to a story Nolie was telling. "I'd hate to think any of our crew wouldn't feel they could be anything they wanted to be, if they worked hard enough."

"Wait for it," Terry murmured as Gabe and Seth came over to join the conversation. "You're about to see the Flanagan juggernaut in action."

He turned toward her, grateful to see a friendly smile. Whatever had almost happened in the barn, Terry either hadn't noticed or was willing to ignore. As he should. "Juggernaut?"

"They tease me about my crusades, but they're just as bad. Listen to them."

Terry was right. The conversation had become general, with people throwing in ideas about how they could help the Ortiz family, and Manuela in particular.

"Are they always like that?" he said softly, just for the pleasure of seeing Terry smile, seeing her gaze go soft with affection for her family.

"Always. Trust me, they're born meddlers, all of them."

A shaft of sunlight, filtered through the leaves of the oak tree, touched Terry's skin, highlighting her freckles and making her green eyes almost golden. He ought to look away—

"So, can we count on you, Jake?" Brendan's question brought him back to earth with a bump.

What had he missed while he was thinking about the color of Terry's eyes? Obviously the question implied that they wanted something from him. "Well, um, what exactly would you want me to do?"

"Just take the opportunity to talk with the girl, that's all. See how serious she is about medicine, what the possibilities are for her. Once we know that, we'll know better if we can do anything to help her."

The last thing he needed was further involvement with the Flanagans and their causes. "Why doesn't Terry talk to her?"

"You're the doctor," Terry said quickly. "Haven't you seen the awe in her face when she looks at you?"

Siobhan was nodding eagerly. "I've tried, but she won't open up to me. I'm sure you're the right person for the job, Jake."

He didn't want to. He didn't have time to. But clearly, he had to agree.

"I'll give it a try, but I'm not promising anything."

Brendan clapped him on the shoulder as if he were a hero, and the others chimed in, talking eagerly about what they might do.

"Juggernaut," Terry murmured. "I told you."

He looked at her, an unwilling smile tugging at his lips. For just a moment understanding flowed between them, strong as the August sun.

He looked away quickly. What had happened to his resolve to stay focused on the job?

Terry grasped the gurney, helping Jeff push through the E.R. doors as the patient continued to protest.

"I'm perfectly all right." The woman clasped her handbag to her chest and glared at Terry. "Just felt a little dizzy, that's all. There's no need for all this fuss."

"Just let the doctor check you out," Terry soothed. "It won't take long." Unless it was the heart attack she suspected, despite the patient's protestations.

Harriet and a nurse joined them the moment they rolled through the doors. She'd already spoken to Harriet on the radio, so the team was ready for their arrival.

"Female, fifty-seven." Terry kept her voice calm for the patient's sake, but instinct told her this was the real thing. She gave the stats quickly. "Experienced shortness of breath, cold sweat and dizziness on her way to work."

"I've just been tired lately, that's all. I haven't been sleeping well. It's nothing."

"Maybe so, but we'd like to be sure of that," Harriet said.

Her gaze met Terry's, and she knew Harriet was thinking the same thing she was—possible heart attack. Too many women didn't realize that their symptoms weren't necessarily the same as a man's. The patient was in good hands with Harriet.

She watched as they headed into the treatment room. Harriet mouthed "good call" over her shoulder as they pushed through the door.

Jeff grinned at her. "Nice job convincing her, Ter. For a while there I thought she was going to hit you with her bag."

"I saw you stayed out of the line of fire," she retorted, hoping Jeff didn't notice the fact that she was glancing around uneasily, hoping not to spot Jake. "You restock while I do the paperwork."

"In a hurry?" He lifted an eyebrow. So he had noticed. They'd been partners since she joined the department, her self-confidence battered by what had happened in Philedelphia. Jeff, with that deceptively laid-back manner and the calm, sure way he had of assuming she knew exactly what to do, had played a big part in helping her bounce back. She'd have adopted him as an older brother, if she didn't already have too many of those.

"Never mind." She grabbed the run report. "Just get us out of here in five minutes, and I'll treat you to coffee."

"Done." Grinning, he headed for the supply room.

Terry leaned on the counter and started filling out the paperwork automatically. She must have been too obvious, if Jeff noticed it. She'd better be more careful.

In the three days since the picnic, she'd managed, through a bit of evasive action, to avoid encountering Jake at all. She just wasn't all that confident of her ability to see him without thinking back to those moments in the barn—moments when she'd been convinced he was going to kiss her.

Well, he hadn't. And she'd behaved perfectly normally for the rest of the picnic, so he couldn't possibly know how embarrassed she'd been.

She smiled and moved a step away as a white-haired hospital auxiliary member set a vase of yellow mums on the counter. Like it or not, she couldn't keep on avoiding Jake forever. She had to get control of her feelings.

Had she been unwittingly sending him signals that day? A flush crept into her cheeks at the thought. Surely not. And yet, why else had it happened? Unless she was completely kidding herself—imagining something that Jake hadn't felt at all.

Somehow she couldn't quite buy that. She'd heard his breath quicken, seen his eyes darken. That had been real.

No matter what Jake had or hadn't felt, one thing was perfectly clear. She couldn't keep telling herself that her feelings were just the remnants of a long-ago crush. She was attracted to the man, despite all the things she disliked about him. Stupid, but whoever said attraction was a rational thing?

She scrawled her signature at the bottom of the run report and handed a copy to the receptionist. Maybe that wasn't what she'd expected to happen at the picnic, but some good had come out of it, too. The family had gotten to know Jake a little, and he'd agreed to help with Manuela. Two positives, to balance one big negative.

Maybe she should stop trying to avoid the man. If she did, perhaps she'd stop blowing his image up in her mind. She could start seeing him as a human being.

She shoved away from the counter. What was taking Jeff so long? There hadn't been that much restocking to do. She crossed the receiving area toward the supply room. She was ready for her morning coffee, even if he wasn't.

She'd nearly reached the door when she saw the stocky figure of her partner heading toward her, empty-handed.

"What's up? Aren't you finished yet?"

He shook his head. "We're finished, all right. We aren't permitted to restock the unit from the hospital supplies any longer."

"What? We've always done that. Who says we can't?"

"I do." Jake came through the door quickly, his lab coat flapping at his movement. His lean face was set, as if he were ready to do battle. "It's a new hospital policy."

"Since when?" She couldn't keep the edge from her voice. "We've always—"

He made a slicing motion with his hand, cutting her off. "It doesn't matter what you've always done, Ms. Flanagan. The E.R. has been directed to cut costs, and that's what we're doing. I'm afraid you'll have to sacrifice along with the rest of us."

That formal use of her name was probably a warning,

reminding her of the difference in their status. Count to five, she warned herself. Better yet, count to ten.

"It hardly seems fair to penalize the paramedics." It took a determined effort to keep her voice calm. "After all, some of our materials stay here, one way or another, every time we deliver a patient."

Something, some small flicker in his eyes, told her she'd scored with that point. Then his mouth tightened.

"Sorry. You can do a direct replacement of any sheets that are left here. That's all."

Generous of him, since otherwise the hospital would end up with all their sheets. "What about other supplies? We always—"

He took a step toward her, his tall form screening her from the interested gazes of the E.R. receptionist, one custodian and two candy stripers who'd paused to watch. "Don't say another word." His voice was low, and those blue eyes were arctic. "Don't push me into a situation where I have to file a complaint about you, Terry. I don't want to do that."

Didn't he? She clamped her lips shut tightly. Could have fooled her on that one. She glared back at him, but in the end, it was her gaze that dropped.

Because like it or not, he was right. She couldn't have an open battle with him in front of staff members, no matter what she felt. She swallowed hard and managed to nod.

All right. When there was no choice, you'd better accept the inevitable as gracefully as possible. Maybe a complaint from the fire chief about the new policy would make Jake reconsider.

She walked quickly toward the door, her partner

closing in behind her as if he couldn't wait to get out of there, either. Whether or not the chief could get this policy reversed, one thing was now clear. Her naive thought that maybe she and Jake could be friends had been blasted to pieces.

By the time she reached the clinic late that afternoon, Terry felt like the ragged end of a rope. They'd done two nursing home transports, gone clear across town on a false alarm, dealt with one combative drunk who'd taken a swing at Jeff, and hauled a reluctant elderly man with a possible broken leg down three flights of stairs. Just another day, but her back ached and the success she'd had with the heart attack patient had receded to the back of a long list.

"You can't get the big save every day," Jeff had commented when he'd headed for his car at the end of the shift. "At least we didn't lose anybody today."

He was right, of course. And she knew herself well enough to know that her irritability wasn't caused by the job. It had its roots in her encounter with Jake.

She pulled into a rutted parking space at the side of the clinic. At least neither of the other two cars already parked there belonged to him. Maybe she could go back to evading the man, since nothing else seemed to work.

She planted a smile on her face and headed for the door. It was nearly five, and experience had shown them that the next couple of hours would be the busy ones, as workers came in from the fields. This was also the first day they were running a bus, borrowed from the church, to the smaller migrant camps in the area, and they had no way of knowing how many people would show up on that.

She paused for a moment as she pulled open the screen door, just to enjoy the sight. What had once been a junk-filled shed now looked like a real clinic. The whitewashed walls and bright lights were the biggest factor, but the small touches her mother had engineered certainly made a difference—bright posters on the wall, a basket of fruit on the desk, a homey braided rug in the waiting area.

Jim Dawson and Carole Peterson, an EMT and a nurse practitioner who had been among her first volunteers, were at the battered desk going over paperwork.

"Hi, Terry." Jim grinned. "I know that aching back stance. How many people did you haul downstairs today?"

She stopped rubbing the small of her back. "Just one, but he weighed enough for three."

Carole waved a form. "If we get anyone from the other camps, should we indicate which one on the intake form?"

"I hadn't thought of that, but it sounds like a good idea. Will you make a note of it on the volunteer hot sheet?"

Carole nodded. The hot sheet had become their lifeline, letting each volunteer know what new issues or solutions had come up during the previous shift. Working with volunteers required a totally different approach from working in the E.R. Had Jake figured that out yet? She doubted it.

The door from the back room swung open, and Manuela hurried through, arms loaded with clean towels. The stack began to tremble, and Terry hurried to help her.

"*Hola,* Manuela. It's good to see you. Are you giving us a hand today?" Maybe this would be a good opportunity to talk to the girl about her hopes, rather than depending on Jake to get around to doing it.

"You didn't know?" Manuela's grin nearly split her face.

Terry blinked. That had to be the first time she'd seen a genuine smile from Manuela, who normally carried more than her fair share of trouble. "Know what?"

"I have a job helping at the clinic. I work every day now. Dr. Jake hired me."

"No. I didn't know." When had all this happened? And why hadn't Jake said anything to her? Surely, as the clinic organizer, she should have been consulted.

Sour grapes, the voice of her conscience commented. You're just jealous because you didn't think of it.

Manuela began stacking towels with as much reverence as if the future of medicine depended on how straight they were. "Dr. Jake came last night to the camp. He talked to me, and he talked to my parents." Her face clouded slightly. "Papa was not sure this was a good thing, but Dr. Jake is paying me more than I could make in the fields, so he agreed."

"That's wonderful." She forced warmth into her voice. Of course she was happy for the girl, and she had to admit, it was an inspired idea. If Manuela did have the makings of a medical professional, they'd find out. "We certainly can use you."

"You will show me how to do things, won't you, Terry? I want to do everything perfectly."

For wonderful Dr. Jake's sake, no doubt. "Of course I will." She gave the girl a quick hug. "We'll make a paramedic out of you yet. Or do you have your sights set on something else?"

"That would be great, to help people the way you do. But I don't think it will be possible. Papa says I must remember that we will be leaving in a few weeks." She smoothed her hand over the surface of a towel. "This won't last."

Terry's throat tightened. Manuela deserved her chance, and she was a jerk for feeling irritated just because it came from someone else.

"No matter how long you're here, you'll learn a lot. Once you've learned something, nobody can take that away. It will go with you wherever you are."

Manuela nodded happily. "And I have Dr. Jake to thank for it."

She kept the smile pinned to her face with an effort. Maybe she'd better go and inventory supplies before she blurted out something she shouldn't about Manuela's new hero.

The storeroom was clean, quiet, and well-organized. Taking the clipboard that hung inside the door, she began checking supplies, jotting down notes as to anything they might need.

Unfortunately, that just reminded her of the episode with the supplies at the hospital. Really, how did Jake expect them to do their work, when—

Okay, enough. She was letting the man take over her thoughts far too much.

Forgive me, Father. I'm obsessing about something I can't control. And I'm actually envious that Jake thought of a way to help Manuela and I didn't. Please, forgive me.

There, she'd said it. Unfortunately she knew perfectly well that there was another step she had to take. She had to thank him for thinking of this gift for Manuela, to say nothing of the fact that he was undoubtedly paying her out of his own pocket. Even if they disagreed on other things, in this he deserved credit.

And she'd have a chance to make good on her decision, because she could hear his voice in the other room. Squaring her shoulders, she marched through the door.

Jake stood at the desk, talking with Carole and Jim. In jeans and a rugby shirt, he looked considerably more casual than he had at the E.R. that morning, but no less intimidating. He didn't turn, but she thought his shoulders stiffened when she approached.

The words didn't seem to be coming, but fortunately for her, the bus pulled up just then. Word of the clinic's work must be spreading through the camps, because at least twenty people began filing through the door.

Thank You, Lord, she murmured silently, and hurried forward to begin triage, as Manuela rushed to translate. *Thank You for giving us this opportunity to help.*

An hour later, things had calmed down considerably. She found herself assisting Jake as he stitched a cut on the forehead of an elderly field worker. She watched his precise, even stitches and tried to find the words she had to say. She may as well blurt it right out.

"I wanted to say—"

He glanced at her, and she was momentarily thrown off her stride by the frosty edge in his gaze.

She cleared her throat. "You're doing a great thing for Manuela. I know she appreciates it. And I do, too." She shouldn't sound so reluctant. "I wish I'd thought of it."

"The important thing is that it happens, not who thought of it." His voice was cool.

"I know that." At least, she knew it rationally, if not emotionally. "She's so excited, and she really is an asset.

I just—I know you must be paying her out of your own pocket. Maybe I can get some donations—"

"Forget it. I can handle it."

"Right. Okay." She took a breath. Of course he could handle it. He probably had a sizable trust fund backing up whatever he decided to do. It must be nice to be able to give without feeling a pinch.

Or was it? She handed him the dressing. Did it mean more when what you gave pinched you a bit? She hadn't given that any thought before, but it was something to ponder. Jesus had certainly thought more of the poor woman who'd given her last two pennies than the rich who gave out of their abundance.

Jake finished the job, nodded in satisfaction, and turned to her as the patient moved away. "You don't think much of me, do you, Terry?"

She fumbled the tray, nearly knocking over the antiseptic. "I don't know what you mean. I just told you how much I appreciate what you're doing for Manuela."

"Did you?" His smile was wry. "Somehow I had the feeling you were thinking something else."

She took a deep breath. She needed to do this right. "I know we've had our share of disagreements." That was putting it mildly. "But you've gone the extra mile for Manuela, and I'm grateful."

He looked at her for a long moment, as if measuring the depth of her sincerity. Then he nodded, and his face seemed to relax a little. "Look, I think we need to clear the air about what happened earlier."

For an instant she thought he meant those moments in the barn, and panic swept through her. Then she realized that he must be talking about the incident at the E.R.

"If we're clearing the air, I have to go on record that I think your new policy is wrong."

"I think it's wrong, as well."

She could only gape at him. "Then why are you doing it?"

Again that wry smile. "Do you really think I have free rein with what happens in the E.R.?"

"Why not? You're the boss, aren't you?"

"It's not that simple." He frowned, and she had the sense that he was choosing his words carefully. "I'd like this position to become permanent, but in order for that to happen, I have to please a lot of people. And one of them happens to be very concerned with cutting costs in the E.R."

"Morley. I know. But why—"

"But surely it doesn't have to be your program that feels the pinch?" His eyebrows lifted.

"I didn't mean that, exactly." Hadn't she?

"I'm going to have to do some things I don't want to do, I'm afraid. I'm willing to take the heat for that." His gaze held hers. "But I'd like to know you'd give me the benefit of the doubt, at least some of the time. What do you say?"

What could she say, especially when he was looking at her as if what she thought really mattered to him?

"All right." She couldn't seem to look away from his face, and she didn't want to think about what that betrayed about her feelings. "I promise."

Chapter Seven

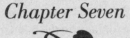

"There you go, sweetheart." Terry smiled at the tot who'd just received her immunization, getting a shy grin in return. The child might not understand what she'd said, but she did understand the red lollipop Terry passed out as a reward for getting immunizations up to date.

The little girl skipped away. The next child in line looked at her lollipop, screwed up his face and edged toward the chair. Terry guided him into place gently.

"This would be a lot easier if we had Manuela here to translate," she said, passing the premeasured immunization to Jake.

He nodded, frowning a little, and then replacing the frown with a grin as he approached the child. *"Hola, amigo."* He darted a glance at Terry. "That's the extent of my Spanish, I'm afraid. Is this the first time Manuela has missed a shift?"

"She's always here waiting when we open the doors. I don't understand it." She glanced toward the door, but no Manuela appeared, eager and smiling. "I hope nothing's wrong."

"We can check on her later if she doesn't show up." He knelt next to the child, and she watched as he deftly gave the injection.

"You know, we can take care of the immunizations if you have something else to do."

She'd called in plenty of volunteers for the immunization day, not knowing how many children would show up. More than she'd have imagined, by the looks of it. Brendan had organized the bus service, and they'd advertised at all the camps.

"Don't I give the injections well enough to suit an experienced paramedic like you?" His eyebrows lifted, but she could see he wasn't really offended. Their truce had held for almost a week, which had to be a record.

"You're doing fine," she assured him. "I just meant it seems like a waste to have a neurosurgeon give childhood immunizations."

"I'm not that any longer." He said the words without any particular inflection, giving no clue to his feelings. "Besides, it's always good to keep your skills sharp." He ruffled the child's hair and sent him to Terry for his lollipop.

"Like Seth over there, trying to remember his high-school Spanish." She nodded toward the sign-in desk, where volunteers tried to take histories and determine what immunizations each child needed.

"He's giving it a valiant effort, I must say. But we could use Manuela there, speaking of skills."

They'd set up three immunization stations, but the slowdown at the sign-in desk meant they had a short break between clients. "Yes, we could. I had some volunteers from the advanced Spanish class at the high school, but I didn't think we'd need them today. By the time I realized we needed them, I couldn't get them out here in time." She welcomed the next mother and child pair. "I wish I knew what happened to Manuela."

Jake knelt next to the little boy, who'd tensed up enough to guarantee the shot would hurt. "Hey, come on, buddy. Relax." He put his stethoscope in the boy's ears. "Want to listen to your heart?" While the boy's attention was distracted, he deftly gave the injection.

"Now that's skill," Terry said, smiling at the child. "No tears at all."

"Glad you appreciate it." Jake straightened.

"Hey, I always appreciated your skill, even back when you were the high-and-mighty neurosurgery consult and I was just another nameless EMT." Too late, she realized she shouldn't have mentioned that again.

But he didn't seem bothered, glancing up from the chart with a slight smile. "Trust me, you were never nameless. An EMT with that mop of red curls could only be called Flanagan. You lit up that place like a torch every time you walked in."

She was absurdly pleased at the comment. "Frankly, I never considered the red hair an asset."

"Combined with that air of naive innocence, it was unmistakable."

Now that wasn't a compliment, although it was true. She'd been decades younger in experience and outlook when she'd arrived in Philadelphia. Eager to prove herself, thinking she had everything under control. She hadn't.

"Terry?" Jake was looking at her, eyes frowning. "What's wrong?"

"Nothing." She forced a smile. "I'd just resent that if

I didn't know it was probably true. I gave a new meaning to *green* then."

She couldn't go any deeper than that, because it led into places that would hurt both of them and destroy this fragile balance. If he didn't realize how bruised she'd been when she'd run back to Suffolk, so much the better.

He was looking at her as if he might pursue the subject, but fortunately she spotted Manuela, hovering outside the screen door. "There's Manuela. Why is she standing out there?"

"Let's find out." Jake started toward the clinic door, and she hurried after him.

The moment she got close enough to see Manuela's face, she knew something was very wrong. No tears— just a set, despairing expression that was somehow worse than tears.

"Manuela, what is it?" She caught the girl's arm, but she stood stiffly, not yielding. "What's wrong?"

Jake guided them away from the clinic door, under the shade of the sycamore tree that stood at the building's corner. "We were worried about you when you didn't come in today," he said quietly. "What happened?"

"I cannot come." Manuela seemed to force the words out. "I just came to tell you that I must not work for the clinic any longer."

"If this is because of your father—"

The girl swallowed hard, shaking her head. "No. Not my father's doing."

Further questions hovered ready to burst from her, but Jake shook his head warningly. "Just tell us in your own way," he said. "Whatever it is, we'll help you."

"You can't help. I should have known—" She stopped, gulping back a sob.

Terry's heart twisted. Known what? That this small thing was too good to be true?

Manuela took a deep breath, straightening her shoulders as if to say she could bear whatever she had to. "The crew chief came to see us."

A ripple of anger rushed through Terry. She should have realized they weren't finished with that man yet. "What is he trying now?"

"Not him." The girl shook her head. "He just brought the message. He said to my father that Mr. Dixon was angry with us. That it was illegal for me to work at the clinic."

She exchanged glances with Jake over the girl's head. Why would Dixon get involved in this? Manuela's family wasn't here illegally, and surely they weren't breaking any laws by paying Manuela for doing chores around the clinic. It wasn't as if she were working long hours or handling dangerous materials.

"Why illegal?" Jake asked. "Did he say why Mr. Dixon thought that?"

"Mr. Dixon said that our contract that allowed us to be here to work was with them. That we must not work for anyone else. He was very angry, so my father says I must not come anymore." She tried for a brave smile, but it trembled. "I thank you for helping me to learn. I'm sorry."

She started to turn away, but Terry grasped her arm, mind racing a mile a minute. "Wait a minute, Manuela. I'm not at all sure he's right about that. We can do something. Jake, tell her."

"I'd like to help, but I don't know what we can do." His gaze evaded hers.

It didn't matter. She knew what he was thinking. That if this came to the hospital board's attention, it would reflect on him. It had been his idea.

"We can't sacrifice Manuela's future for the sake of expediency."

Jake met her eyes now, his look level. "It's not a question of expediency."

Jake had a job at stake, so he said. Maybe she couldn't believe his position really hinged on something so trivial, but she had to respect that. Still, her hands weren't tied.

"Look, I can understand why you might not want to be involved." She kept her voice even. This didn't have to lead to a fight. They could talk about it like colleagues, not enemies. "You can stay out of it. I'll go to see Matthew Dixon myself."

"No." His fingers closed over her arm. Before she could jerk away, he spoke again. "*You're* not going to see Matthew Dixon. *We* are."

In the few minutes it took to drive over the back roads to the Dixon farmhouse, Jake managed to second-guess himself at least thirty times. Did he really want to do this? What if Dixon turned around and complained to the chief of staff about him? Or worse, complained to Morley?

The lane curved around a clump of sumac bushes, their plumes red as flames, and the house came into view. A brick center section, its color worn to a soft rose over probably a couple of centuries, had wings of white frame going out on either side. A generous porch spanned the front.

The house should look welcoming, but instead it seemed faintly forlorn. The lane was rutted, and the porch sagged a bit at one end. No flowers filled the beds to either side of the front walk, and a crumbling brick wall enclosed what had probably been a side garden.

"They could use a load of gravel," Terry commented as they bumped to a stop.

"It looks as if Mr. Dixon hasn't been keeping the place up very well." He sat with his hands on the wheel, staring at the house. "Is he badly off?"

Terry shrugged. "I'm not sure any farmers are doing really well now, but Dixon has always been thought to have plenty of family money. I remember that Andy and his sisters went away to a private academy when the rest of us headed to Suffolk Middle School."

He glanced at her. Terry's temper had nearly gotten the better of her at Manuela's tale, but she seemed to have it under control now. She was frowning a little, her forehead crinkling and her green eyes clouded.

"So, did you miss him when he went away?"

Her wide-eyed gaze met his. "Andy? Get serious."

"He said you were his girlfriend." Even in this situation, he couldn't resist the urge to tease her a little. Was that what all those siblings of hers did?

"I don't know why he was goofing off like that. He barely noticed me when we were in elementary school. Girls weren't big on his agenda then."

"What was?"

"Sports, I guess. And having the best of everything. Whatever the new fad was, Andy had to have it first."

"Seems funny he settled down here again after school. You'd have expected him to head for the bright lights." The way Terry had. Did she regret coming back to Suffolk?

Her mouth firmed a little, almost as if she guessed what he thought. "I suppose Andy felt his father needed him. This is a big operation." She glanced toward the barn. It needed a coat of paint, too. "Or at least, it was. If Matthew Dixon is having financial troubles, that could account for the condition of the workers' housing. Well, are we going in?" She grasped the door handle.

"Wait a second." His hand brushed her shoulder. "When we get in there, let me handle talking to Mr. Dixon."

He could feel her tense through that lightest of contacts, her shoulder tightening against his fingers.

"Why?" She sounded ready for battle. "My family has known him for years."

And you're the stranger here. She didn't add that, but she was probably thinking it.

"That didn't seem to help you the last time you confronted him, did it?"

Her frown deepened. "That was odd, now that I think about it. I'd have expected him to recognize me as a Flanagan, even if he didn't remember my name. I guess I'm not as memorable as I thought."

He let his finger touch a strand of coppery hair. "Maybe it's not that. Have there been any rumors about Dixon's health?"

"Not that I know of." Her gaze met his. "Are you thinking some form of dementia?"

"It's possible. That might explain the son's protective attitude."

She nodded slowly. "I guess so. Brendan might know

something, as their pastor, but he wouldn't say. Maybe we ought to talk to Andy, instead."

"Manuela said the orders came from the old man. Let's start with him, in any event." He opened the door. "I don't suppose you'd consider waiting in the car?"

"No, I wouldn't."

She slid out, and he rounded the car to join her. They mounted the three steps to the porch, their footsteps thudding in the silence. The glass-paneled door stood open behind the barrier of a flimsy screen door.

He knocked, the door rattling in its frame. Nothing. He tried again, harder. A voice, sounding far away, called something he couldn't distinguish. He glanced at Terry.

"Do you suppose that meant come in?"

"Let's take it that way."

She yanked the screen door open and stepped inside. He followed her into a center hallway, papered in a floral pattern that looked as if it would have been right at home in the 1930s. A staircase mounted to the second floor, and archways on either side of them led into a living room and dining room furnished with dark, heavy pieces.

"Mr. Dixon?" Terry called. "Are you here?"

This time they got a livelier response. A door at the back of the hallway swung open, and Andy Dixon strode through. He checked his steps momentarily at the sight of them and then came forward, smiling, his hand extended.

"Terry. Dr. Landsdowne. This is an unexpected pleasure. What can I do for you?"

Impatient, Jake cut across Terry's polite response. "We'd like to speak to your father, please."

Andy's open face clouded, and he glanced toward the

second floor. "I'm afraid you can't. He always rests in the afternoon. Can't I help you with whatever it is?"

"We'd prefer to talk with him." He glanced at his watch. Nearly five. "Won't he be getting up soon?"

"I'm afraid not." Andy's voice lowered, and he took a step closer to them. "The truth is, he's not up to handling much of anything these days. So if you need something, I'm afraid you'll have to make do with me."

"We're worried about Manuela. Manuela Ortiz." Terry burst into speech. "Mel Jordan told her parents that your father objected to her working at the clinic."

He should have known Terry wouldn't be able to stay out of it. "We've been paying Manuela a small amount to help out," he explained. "It's useful to have her to translate to the patients, and we couldn't understand why your father would object to that."

"This must be some sort of misunderstanding. Look, let's go out on the porch and talk. I don't want to risk Dad hearing. He gets upset over nothing these days."

He ushered them out onto the porch. Giving them a very polite version of the bum's rush? Jake couldn't help but wonder how the Dixon family's chain of command fit together. Was Andy really in charge, as he seemed to imply?

"That's better." Andy closed the door behind them, his pleasant face creased with worry. "Really, I'm sorry about this. Of course there's no problem with the girl— Manuela, is it?—working at the clinic."

"Apparently Jordan thought there was." He didn't care to be caught in the middle over who was in charge here.

"Jordan has no business speaking to my father at

all." Andy's voice sharpened. "I've told him that. Please don't worry about it. I'll take care of everything."

"Thank you, Andy." Terry's voice was warm, and she seemed to accept everything the man said at face value. There was no reason why that should annoy him, but it did.

"I'd just like to be certain that your father isn't going to complain about us to the hospital."

"Believe me, I'll make sure that doesn't happen." Andy glanced at his watch. "I don't want to rush you, but I do have some things to do—"

"Of course." Terry shot him a look that demanded politeness. "We're very grateful, Andy. And Manuela will be so relieved."

"Yes. Thank you."

"My pleasure." Lifting his hand in farewell, Andy went back into the silent farmhouse, closing the door firmly behind him.

Terry frowned at him. "What's wrong? We got what we wanted. You should be happy."

"I am. It's fine." He started toward the car. It was fine, wasn't it? So why did he have this nagging worry that the situation with the Dixons could explode in his face?

Jake stood for the final blessing as the worship service ended. Brendan, formal in his black robe, spread his arms wide, as if to embrace the entire congregation of Grace Church. Jake felt himself giving in to the warmth and tried to resist. Then the organ music swelled, and Brendan was walking quickly to the back toward the sanctuary.

Jake slid the hymnal back into its rack. He still wasn't

sure why he'd come to worship this morning. Maybe it should be credited, or debited, to Brendan's persistence. He could hardly tell Brendan that he preferred to do his wrestling with God in private these days. Maybe he could leave—

But Siobhan Flanagan slipped through the pews, slim and agile as a girl, to cut him off. "Jake, how nice to see you this morning. How did you like the service?"

It was impossible to resist the warmth of her smile. "Very much. Brendan is an excellent speaker." He'd rather talk about Brendan's speaking ability than the topic of the sermon.

"…we are called to do the good work God has already prepared for us to do," Siobhan quoted. "That's one of my favorite verses."

"It seems a rather frightening one to me." The words came out before he had a chance to remind himself that he didn't intend to open up about his private spiritual health.

"Why?" Her air of interested attention robbed the word of any intent to pry.

"I suppose because it puts a heavy burden on the individual. If you don't do the work God planned for you, who will?"

"True. But I always see it that since God planned it, He also prepares us to do it." Her smile flashed. "Well, enough serious theology for the moment. Let's go to Fellowship Hall before all the coffee is gone."

She linked her arm in his, clearly not taking no for an answer. He let her draw him into the flow of people heading out the door to the left of the pulpit.

He wouldn't argue with Siobhan, but he wasn't sure

she was right. He'd thought he'd known what God wanted of him, but either he'd been wrong or God had changed His mind.

Fellowship Hall was an expanse of beige carpet and beige cinder block walls, brightened by colorful banners between the windows. The buzz of conversation was nearly deafening. It sounded as if these people hadn't seen each other in weeks.

Siobhan tugged him directly to a serving table laden with cookies, coffee cake, fruit, cheese, even vegetables and dip. A person could make a meal of what was spread out for the coffee hour, and it looked as if some people were.

Well, he'd have his coffee and speak to a few people, so no one could accuse him of being unfriendly.... Now why did a certain redhead's face pop into his mind at that thought?

Siobhan had been caught by an elderly woman who seemed intent on volunteering her for a rummage sale, so he took a few steps away, scanning the crowd. Somewhat to his surprise, he saw a few people from the migrant camp. Perhaps Brendan had sent the bus for them. They'd been corralled by a smiling couple and ushered to the food table as if they were the guests of honor.

When he spotted Terry's red curls, he realized he'd been looking for her. A niece and a nephew hung from each hand, and she was laughing down at them.

Something warm seemed to unfurl in his heart at her expression. Terry, of all people, ought to be married with children of her own by now. They'd look like her, with those red curls and green eyes.

Terry's gaze met his, and now the smile was for him. He couldn't leave without speaking to her. He'd just say hello, and then he'd be free to leave. He made his way through the crowd to her side.

"Looks as if you have an anchor on each arm," he said.

"I have a pest on each arm," she said with mock ferocity. "Go on, you two. Go get another cookie. Your mom will really appreciate the sugar high."

They ran off. She watched them for a moment before turning to him. "Is everything all right?"

"Of course. Why wouldn't it be?" She couldn't know he found it difficult to be here.

"I thought you might have run into Matthew Dixon. He hardly ever comes to church, but he's here today."

He glanced around the room. "Maybe I should speak to him. Where is he?"

"Over there." She drew in a breath. "He's talking to Dr. Getz. I'm not sure that's a good idea."

"I'm sure it's not," he said grimly. "I suppose I should see just what they're talking about."

"If he's complaining, it's probably about me. I'll come, too."

He almost told her he'd handle it, but they weren't in the hospital now. This was her turf, not his. Besides, for some ridiculous reason it felt good to have someone next to him as he approached the two men.

"It's been terrible, that's what it's been." Dixon, lean as a rail in a navy suit that looked as if it didn't get much use, glared at Sam Getz.

Jake felt as if he'd been punched. Dixon was complaining about them to the chief of staff. How was he going to explain this away?

"It was that late frost," Getz said. He glanced at them with a smile. "Not that Dr. Landsdowne would know what a late frost does to the apple harvest. He's a city boy."

Dixon gave Jake a short nod, his eyes a little uncertain, as if not sure he knew him.

"Dr. Landsdowne is in charge of the clinic," Terry said. "And I'm Terry Flanagan. Remember me?"

"Joe Flanagan's girl. 'Course I remember you. Didn't I see you someplace lately?"

The old man was failing, obviously. More surprising was the fact that his son had let him out alone. But even as he thought that, he spotted Andy working his way through the crowd, balancing two coffee cups.

He could only be relieved. Dixon didn't apparently remember anything about the situation with Manuela. Or at least, didn't know that he and Terry had interceded. Presumably Andy was handling the situation.

Getz clapped him on the shoulder, startling him. "I'll tell you why I wanted this young man to head up our emergency services, Matt. He gave up an important position to work in an African medical mission. Anybody who'd do that has his priorities in the right place."

He froze. He couldn't look at Terry. She knew why he'd really gone. If Getz found out, he'd lose that respect for Jake's priorities in a hurry.

"I guess somebody has to do it." Dixon's voice was grudging. "I wouldn't want to go rushing off to Africa."

Jake gave him a meaningless smile. All he could think was that he wanted to get out of here.

But Getz's hand still clasped his shoulder. "You know, hard as it is to believe, I was actually in medical school with Jake's father. He went on to fame and fortune, and I'm right back here where I grew up. Funny world, isn't it?"

Funny wasn't the word for it. His stomach was churning, the coffee turning to acid. Getz. And his father. There couldn't be a worse combination.

It's a coincidence. Stop overreacting. No one here knows about your relationship with your father. No one ever will.

But Terry was looking at him with concern in her face, and he was afraid she was beginning to read him entirely too well.

Chapter Eight

Terry glanced out one of the small windows at the clinic. The sky was dark with low clouds, the air so heavy it was almost hard to breathe. The narrow lane that led toward the migrant housing lay dusty and empty.

Manuela sat in one of the metal chairs in the waiting area, bent over the heavy book in her lap. Her long hair, loose today, hung down over her shoulders like a curtain, and she twisted a lock around her finger.

"Looks like we're not getting any customers today." She slid onto the chair next to the girl, the metal clammy to the touch. "We may as well close up early."

Manuela seemed to come back from a long way away. "*¿Que?* Oh, yes, I see." She closed the book slowly. "I'm sorry if I am wasting time. Do you want me to do something?"

"Reading isn't wasting time. Are you studying something for school?"

Her dark lashes swept down, hiding her eyes. "Not exactly. I'm not in school."

"Well, not now, I guess. But school will start next week." Hard to believe the summer was over already. The days had been flying by since she'd been busy with the clinic.

"I won't be going." Longing showed in her face for a brief moment. "My father says we won't bother to start school here, since we will be leaving in a few weeks."

"I see." Tread carefully, she warned herself. You don't really know what life is like for Manuela. "You're studying on your own, then."

Manuela drew her hands away to show her the cover of the book she held. It was a tenth grade biology text. "Your mother got this book for me. So I could try to keep up with my studies. She says if I want to go into a medical field, I must do well in science."

Trust Mom to come up with some practical way to help Manuela. Guilt pricked at her. She'd been so preoccupied with the clinic that she hadn't followed through on her intention to do more to help Manuela realize her dreams.

"I'm glad she did that. Isn't it hard to study something like science in English?"

"Something that's hard is worth doing. Besides, I love it." She flipped open the book to a chart showing a diagram of the human body. "Look. This shows how the blood travels in the body, and there's another that shows how the heart works."

"I wish I'd been that enthusiastic about learning things when I was your age." Manuela should have her chance to achieve. If only she could stay long enough to get some uninterrupted schooling…. "Isn't it possible for your family to stay a bit longer, so you can start school here?"

She shrugged. "Some workers will stay through the

fall, to work the fruit harvest, but so far my father has not been chosen."

"Who decides that?" She was beginning to have a bad feeling about this.

Manuela didn't look at her. "The farmer says how many workers he needs. The crew chief gets to pick."

And Jordan wouldn't pick her father, that was what she didn't say. Because Terry had made too many waves. It had never occurred to her that Jordan had the power to retaliate against the Ortiz family.

"I see." She suppressed the words that sprang to her lips. She couldn't hold out false hope to the girl. "If Mr. Dixon wanted your father to stay, would he?"

Manuela nodded. "But it's up to Mr. Jordan."

"Maybe so. But maybe Mr. Dixon would intercede with him."

"If you asked him?" Manuela's eyes shone. "Would you, Terry?"

"I'm not sure he'd listen to me, but maybe if my cousin Brendan talked to him." She put her hand over the girl's. She didn't want to encourage Manuela too much, but surely a little hope was good for her. "Would you like to go to school here?"

"More than anything. I'm always so far behind when I am able to attend school." Manuela's fingers clung to hers. "If I could do well in school, maybe I could be a paramedic, like you, and help people." Her tone made that dream sound as faraway as the moon.

"If that's what you want, I'm sure you could. Let me talk to Brendan and see if there's anything he can do, okay?" Brendan wanted to find some specific way to help the Ortiz family. This might be it.

Raindrops spattered against the windowpane, startling her. "Uh-oh. Looks like the storm is coming. Maybe you'd better run home."

Manuela jumped up. "My mother will be worried." She slid the book onto the high shelf that ran above the chairs. "I'll leave the book here, where it will be safe. Thank you, Terry."

She turned and darted out the door, running down the path toward the cement block building that was her temporary home.

There was no point in wondering what the girl had meant about leaving her book here so it would be safe. Maybe she just hadn't wanted to risk getting it wet.

Now she was the one who'd better hurry. The narrow road that twisted its way to the clinic was barely passable at the best of times. During a hard rain, it would be downright dangerous.

She started through her checklist for closing up the clinic, trying not to listen to the spatter of rain on the tin roof. Just a few more things, and she could leave.

The sound of a car engine distracted her. She wasn't expecting any of her volunteers at this hour. But it was Jake who hurried through the door, the shoulders of his navy windbreaker sparkling with raindrops.

"No customers?" He lifted his eyebrows.

Are you checking up on me, Jake? Despite the fact that their relationship had eased in recent days, it was impossible not to think that.

"It's been a quiet afternoon, so I sent Manuela home. I was just trying to get out myself before the storm hit." She picked up the clipboard. "Do you want to see today's records?"

He moved toward her, slipping the wet jacket off and tossing it over the desk chair. "Anything unusual?" He glanced quickly through the entries.

"Nothing much." Lightning cracked, and her nerves seemed to jump in response. "The road gets pretty bad in a storm, so maybe we should go—"

Another lightning crack, a boom of thunder, and the skies opened up. Rain poured down, thundering on the tin roof so loudly that it deafened her until her ears adjusted to the sound. Water streamed down the windows and turned the trees to a deep, iridescent green. The dirt clearing in front of the clinic changed in moments to glistening mud.

Rain and wind rattled the screen door, and Jake hurried to close the heavy inner door. He gave her a rueful look. "Sorry. If I hadn't interrupted you, you might have gotten out before this hit."

"Or I might have been sliding off the hill into the gully about now." She shrugged. "I'm afraid we're stuck for the moment."

"Sorry," he said again. "That wasn't my intent in stopping by. Is there any coffee left in the pot?"

She nodded, starting toward it, but he got there first and poured his own.

"Some for you?" He lifted the pot, looking at her questioningly.

For a moment, she couldn't seem to respond. In jeans and a blue polo shirt, his hair ruffled from the rain, Jake looked far too approachable for her peace of mind. Concentrate, she ordered herself fiercely. Don't act like some sort of medical groupie.

"No, thanks." Thank goodness her voice sounded casual. "I drink too much of that stuff when I'm on duty."

He nodded, taking a mouthful and making a face. "Every first responder I've ever known has been the same."

"I'd argue at that sweeping statement, but I'm afraid you're right. If my partner had his way, we'd stop for coffee and doughnuts after every call."

A gust of wind sent rain clattering against the window. Something—a branch, maybe—hit the roof with a crash. She shivered and rubbed her arms, despite the fact that it wasn't really cold.

Jake crossed the room to her, leaning against the desk next to her, and his nearness had her nerves standing at attention. "Are you cold?"

"No. Just never too fond of being out in the middle of nowhere in a storm." She took a breath. Maybe she could turn the fact of being stuck here to good account. "Speaking of paramedics, Manuela told me this afternoon that she'd like to become one. I'd love to clear the way to get the training for her, when she's old enough."

Jake frowned at the muddy liquid in his mug and set it down on the desk. "She's a bright girl. Maybe she ought to aim higher than that."

For a moment, she couldn't respond at all. Really, she didn't need to worry about feeling too attracted to him, since he managed to make her furious on a regular basis. She shoved herself away from the desk.

"Aim higher? Meaning that paramedics are at the bottom of the totem pole, as far as you're concerned."

"That's not exactly what I said."

He wouldn't think of apologizing, of course.

"Paramedics are on the front lines in medical emergencies. We go into situations other professionals never dream of, and we help people at the time of their greatest crisis." She shouldn't have to defend her profession to Jake, of all people.

Suddenly it hit her, like a blow to the stomach. The words Jake had spoken in the aftermath of Meredith's death seemed to ring in her ears. "Or maybe it's just me you don't want Manuela to emulate. Maybe you think she shouldn't aim to follow a poor excuse for a medical professional like me."

Jake could only stare at Terry. This storm between them had blown up more suddenly than the one that battered the building from outside. Could he possibly pretend he didn't know what she was talking about?

He put the cup aside, the coffee turning to acid in his stomach. No. He couldn't ignore this. He owed Terry more than that.

"Did I say that to you?" It took an effort to keep his gaze on hers.

"Yes. Don't you remember?" She'd taken a few steps away from him, and she stood braced, her hands tensed into fists as if ready for a fight.

"I remember saying some things I shouldn't have when I—" he stopped, swallowed "—when I realized Meredith was dead."

Pain flickered in her face. "You meant what you said. That she might have lived if a more experienced crew had responded to the call."

He shoved his hand through his hair. His head was starting to pound with the effort of revisiting those memories. "I don't know what I meant, Terry. You must have had patients' families lash out at you before this. It may not be pretty, but it happens."

"It's a lot more serious when a doctor does the lashing out." Her eyes flickered. "I've been through worse things than that inquiry, but not many."

He shook his head, his throat tightening. "You shouldn't have had to go through that. I know. But it was all right. Your team was cleared. You didn't suffer any consequences from it."

Her eyes widened. "No consequences? Only that it sent me scurrying back to Suffolk with my tail between my legs. But I'm sure that's what you intended."

Had he intended that? He'd just known he hadn't wanted to see her again in his hospital. But then, it hadn't stayed his hospital for long, had it?

"I'm sorry." He had to force the words out. "It wasn't fair to you. I know." The words he'd never said to anyone hovered on his lips, wanting to be released.

"Then why?" Her face twisted, and he realized that she was still hurting. "Why did you blame us? It wasn't our fault."

"No." He knew then he'd have to say it. Terry was the one person in the world he couldn't pretend to about this. "It wasn't your fault Meredith died. It was mine."

The words seemed to echo in the shocked silence between them. There was no sound but the drumming of the rain. That, and his own ragged breathing.

"Why?" The word sounded strangled. "Why was it your fault?"

He rubbed the back of his neck, where the tension was building. It didn't help. "You deserve to hear this, don't you? You're the one who was caught in the fallout of my mistakes. What did you know about Meredith?"

"Just what everyone knew. That she was a Main Line socialite. That she was crazy about you. That you two were going to be married."

He shook his head. There it was again—he'd never understood how that misperception had flown through the hospital. "We weren't. I dated her, yes. My sister had known her at school, had introduced us. But it was never that serious between us."

"Everyone said it was." Terry watched him, eyes serious, as if weighing his words for truth.

"The notorious hospital grapevine, in other words." He leaned back against the desk, trying to relax the tension that rode him. "That's really a reliable source."

Something flared in her gaze. "It wasn't my only source. She—Meredith—she said that, the first time we were called to her apartment. That we should take her to General, because her fiancé was a resident there."

He was smothering again, caught in the lies Meredith had spun around them. "Terry, I'm asking you to believe me. I never asked Meredith to marry me. I never had anything more than a brief, casual relationship with her."

"Then why did she say that?"

She wasn't going to believe him unless he told her everything, and he wasn't sure he could. He shook his head slowly.

"Look, I'm still not sure how it happened. We went out a few times. I enjoyed it. Going out with her was a link to my old world, a break from the hospital. But it didn't take long to figure out that there was no future for us. She was completely uninterested in everything that was important to me—my work, my patients, my future. I knew I had to break it off before it got serious."

"She thought it was already serious," Terry said.

It wasn't much, but it was a faint indication that she might understand. "She didn't listen to me. She kept calling me, even at the hospital. I couldn't seem to make her understand."

He remembered, too well, how his discomfort had given way to irritation and then finally to a yawning fear that Meredith would never accept the truth.

"One night she called." Every instant of that time was engraved on his memory. "She said she couldn't live without me. That she'd taken an overdose of sleeping pills. She was calling to say goodbye."

In the stillness, he heard Terry's breath catch. "Had she really taken an overdose?"

"I was sure she had. I rushed over there, raced her to the emergency room, terrified of not being in time. They pumped the drugs out of her, suggested counseling, which she refused. She said she'd been depressed, foolish, she was all right now. I believed her, probably because I wanted to."

He couldn't easily forgive himself for his stupidity. If he'd insisted on counseling, tried to be her friend… But he hadn't.

"I thought she was all right. Until it happened again. And again. And finally the doctor who treated her broke all the rules out of his pity for me and told me she'd never taken enough to kill herself. Enough to make herself sick. Not enough to kill."

"I'm sorry." Terry's voice was very soft. "Sorry for her. Sorry for you."

Tears shimmered in her eyes, and the warmth that was Terry seemed to reach out and touch him.

"You must have known some of it," he said, trying to keep the pain and shame out of his voice. "You answered the calls a couple of times."

"Yes. But the last time—"

"The last time I was in a meeting. I'd turned my cell phone off. And she'd taken a different medication, one it turned out she was allergic to. By the time your team got there, by the time I knew, it was too late." His throat was so tight he didn't think he could say much more, but one thing had to be said. "It wasn't your fault, Terry. It wouldn't have made any difference who answered that call. The only fault was mine."

Her heart was breaking for him. Terry moved closer, wanting to comfort him, afraid she was the one person who never could. The pain in his voice, his face, was indescribable. The cool, detached, unfeeling man felt only too much.

"It wasn't your fault, Jake. Honestly. You can't blame yourself for turning off your cell phone when you were in a meeting. If you'd known, you'd have gone."

"Would I?" The words sounded bitter, echoing in the quiet room. The rain had subsided to a gentle patter, making a soft background to their voices. "You have more faith in me than I have in myself if you believe that. Maybe I didn't want to get any more of those calls. Maybe I wouldn't have answered even if I'd gotten it."

She knew the answer to that one, even if she couldn't make this better for him. "Yes. You would have."

He blinked, probably at the conviction in her voice. "How do you know that? I'm not sure myself."

"Anyone who knows you would know. Think about it. Not even your worst enemy could accuse you of neglecting a patient, any patient. No matter what. You might have been angry. You might have wanted to be rid of the complications she'd brought into your life. But you would have gone."

"I wish I could be sure." He stared down at his hands—those talented, capable, surgeon's hands. "That keeps me awake at night sometimes."

"It shouldn't." She tried to project all her confidence into her words. "Maybe you can blame yourself for not handling the situation better, but you can't blame yourself for that. You would have gone."

He sent a fleeting glance toward her, and she thought she read hope there. It twisted her heart. She'd thought him so sure, so confident, so fortunate. And all the time he'd been suffering.

"Thank you, Terry." His voice was grave. "It means something to hear you say that."

For a long moment they stood looking at each other, and her breath seemed to stop. They'd come so close to each other in the past few moments. It seemed the barriers between them were gone.

That was an illusion, she told herself desperately. Just as it was an illusion that he was looking at her with a warmth she'd never seen from him before.

Slowly, very slowly, he reached out and touched her hair, pushing a wayward strand back behind her ear with as much concentration as he'd give to a complicated bit of surgery. Her breath seemed to have stopped completely, but her heart was thrumming in her ears.

His fingertips brushed her cheek, warming where they touched. His eyes darkened.

She had to do something, say something. But she couldn't. She could only watch as his face grew nearer and nearer until his lips touched hers.

He didn't attempt to draw her into an embrace. There was nothing but the light pressure of his palm cradling her face, his lips gentle and undemanding on hers.

But there was longing behind that kiss; she knew it and felt the same yearning in herself. Careful, careful. But she couldn't seem to pull away.

He did, finally, drawing back a fraction of an inch, so that she still felt his breath against her lips. His fingertips drew a line down her cheek. And then he stepped away, something rueful in his eyes.

"I shouldn't have done that."

The words were a wake-up call. She shouldn't have, either. She moved back a cautious step, trying to gather whatever shreds she had left of self-possession.

"I—yes, I mean, it wasn't your fault, but it—it probably wasn't a good idea. We have to work together."

It didn't mean anything to you, Jake. And I'm afraid it meant too much to me.

"Besides, you don't like me very much, remember?" His voice had a teasing gentleness that seemed to turn her spine to marshmallow.

"I don't—" Maybe she'd better be careful not to give too much away. "I don't dislike you. Now that I understand what happened…"

The sentence died away, because she saw the difference in Jake's face as she spoke. He seemed to tighten, withdrawing from her, as if moving back behind the shield of the perfect, impersonal surgeon again.

"I'd rather no one else knew about that."

Now it was her turn to stiffen. Did he really know so little of her as to think she'd blab that around?

"I certainly won't say anything." The words sounded just as tight and stiff as she felt.

The moment when they'd stood so close, lips touching, understanding each other without words—it might never have happened. Maybe as far as Jake was concerned, it hadn't.

Well, if that's what he wanted, she could pretend, too. But she couldn't fool herself. He'd kissed her, and her heart was never going to be the same.

Chapter Nine

The next day, Terry turned down the pleasant residential street where Mary Kate and her two children lived, trying to focus on anything except that interlude with Jake. Think about her sister, putting up that bright, impervious facade to hide her grief. Think about the clothes Shawna and Michael had outgrown, that Mary Kate wanted to give the children at the migrant camp. Don't think about Jake.

Well, that certainly wasn't the way to forget, by telling herself to do so. That just brought it surging to the forefront of her mind. She slowed to allow a group of boys tossing a football to clear the tree-lined street. In another week they'd be in school, and this block would be silent and deserted during the day except for a few mothers with strollers.

She bit her lip. Poor Jake. Whoever would have expected her to think that of him, the man she'd thought had everything? Instead, he was carrying a burden of guilt that was nearly crushing him.

What she'd told him was true, if he could only accept it. To think that he wouldn't have answered Meredith's call was ridiculous. No one who knew him in a professional capacity would believe he wouldn't fight to the end of his strength for a patient.

As for what prompted that fight—well, there she wasn't so sure. She'd heard one of the E.R. docs talking once, after having been asked to scrub in on a surgery Jake was performing on a patient they'd treated in the E.R.

"You have to hand it to Landsdowne, like him or not," he'd said. "It wasn't just his skill that saved that patient. It was his will. He wasn't going to let her slip away on his table." Then he'd added, "It'd be a reflection on him if she died. That's what he'd think."

Had that anonymous doc been right? She wasn't sure, but that had certainly been the overall impression he'd left at the hospital—that of a brilliant surgeon who'd taken so much pride in his skill that it was an affront if a patient died.

He wouldn't have let Meredith die, not if he could have saved her. As for the rest of it—well, maybe he hadn't handled the situation as well as he could have. She could well imagine his impatience with Meredith. Still, he couldn't possibly have anticipated the situation going so very wrong.

She pulled slowly into Mary Kate's driveway, watching for abandoned bikes and roller skates. So he probably hadn't handled Meredith as well as he might have. Hadn't seen that she got the help she needed. On the other hand, he hadn't been a relative, just an acquaintance. There were limits to what he could do. And doctors could be just as blind as the next person to psychiatric problems in those closest to them.

Brendan would have handled it differently, but Brendan had unique gifts. She got out of the car, shutting the door and cutting across the grass toward the front door of the white ranch. Mary Kate's coneflowers and chrysanthemums made a splash of yellow and orange against the siding.

Brendan would say that people were given different gifts so that they could come together in the body of Christ and do the work Christ had commissioned. Probably it was wrong to wish her own gifts, or Jake's, had been different. But if she had a bit of Jake's detachment, she might be able to stop feeling a pain in her heart every time she thought of that kiss.

She knocked and opened the door simultaneously, calling out. "Mary Kate? Kids? Anyone here?"

Her sister hurried into the living room from the hall that led to the bedrooms, her arms filled with two large cardboard boxes, her hair disheveled. "Don't shout, Terry. I'm here."

"Sorry." She went to take one of the boxes and realized that Mary Kate's eyes were red and swollen. For a moment, she couldn't speak. "Where do you want this?"

She was relieved to hear her voice coming out normally. Mary Kate never showed her grief to her little sister. Should she say something or ignore it?

Mary Kate took the decision out of her hands, plopping the box on the dining table and wiping her eyes with the back of her hands. "I climbed up in the attic for these. The dust up there made my eyes water." She yanked one of the boxes open. "Let's see what's in here."

So they were supposed to ignore it. She couldn't

help but think there were other things besides the kids' outgrown clothes in the attic—things related to Kenny that might have broken through Mary Kate's iron self-control.

"These were Michael's." Mary Kate was stacking small pairs of jeans and T-shirts on the table. "Do you think they'll fit any of the kids at the camp?"

"They'd be great." She smoothed out a blue shirt decorated with trucks and bulldozers. "This would at least fit Juan Ortiz and I'm sure plenty of others."

"That's the family with the daughter you were talking about at the picnic, isn't it?" Mary Kate paused, hands on the pile of clothing. "Was Jake able to do anything about the girl?"

"Jake?" Mary Kate's casual use of his name startled her, and for a moment she couldn't respond. She gathered her scattered wits. It wouldn't do to let her sister know she had any feelings for him. "Yes. He gave Manuela a job at the clinic. She's done very well there. We're hoping the family can stay through the fall, so she can get in some regular school time."

"Sounds like a nice guy, going to that trouble for her." The comment was accompanied by a sidelong glance from Mary Kate's bright blue eyes.

She swallowed. "He's nice enough." She felt the betraying flush come up in her cheeks and ducked her head, hoping Mary Kate didn't notice.

"Terry!" Mary Kate swung to face her. "Are you involved with him?"

Obviously that hope had been futile. "No, I'm not involved. We work together, that's all."

"You don't blush at the mention of a man just because

you work with him. Come on, out with it." Her voice had that familiar, I'm-the-big-sister, commanding tone.

"There's nothing to tell," she said. "Do you want me to take all these things?"

Mary Kate pushed the clothes out of her hands impatiently. "Quit trying to avoid the subject. I know something's going on. Why won't you be honest with me?"

Her Flanagan temper, never far away, flared at that. "Maybe for the same reason you're not honest with me about your feelings."

"What are you talking about?" Mary Kate's face whitened, her freckles standing out against her fair skin.

"You." Maybe it was time this came out. "You put up this ridiculous, shiny barrier that no one can get through, making the rest of us pretend that everything is just fine. Well, it's not—don't you think I know that?"

Mary Kate's face was dead white now, her eyes blazing. "Of course it's not! Do you think I don't think about Kenny a thousand times every day? And at night—" Her voice broke, tears welling over.

"Oh, honey, I'm so sorry." She reached for Mary Kate, aghast at what her well-meaning meddling had done. "I'm sorry. I know how much you're hurting."

"No, you don't!" Mary Kate shoved her hands away so hard she went back a step. "I pray you never do." She grabbed the boxes, thrusting everything inside and shoving them into Terry's arms. "Take all of it."

"Mary Kate—"

A decisive shake of the head stopped her. "Leave it, okay? I have to deal with this my way. Now just go."

She'd made a mess of things. What on earth had made

her think she could help her sister? When it came to out-of-control emotions, she couldn't even help herself.

Jake tried to concentrate on the charts he was reviewing, but the headache that pressed on his temples and clamped the back of his neck made focusing difficult. Giving up, he slid them back into the chart rack and headed for the break room. The E.R. was late-afternoon still, the only patient a nursing home resident who was being transferred upstairs. The staff could spare him, and caffeine might help his head.

Maybe the headache was the aftermath of yesterday's mistakes. He should never have let things go so far with Terry. He'd blurted out far more than he'd intended about his own affairs. He'd never told anyone that much about what happened with Meredith. Never. His head pounded in time with his footsteps on the tiled floor. It was his burden to carry.

Her confession that she'd fled Philadelphia, considering herself a failure even after the inquiry had cleared her, had shaken him. He should have talked to her about that, tried to draw her out and repair some of the damage he'd done.

Instead, he'd just soaked up all that warmth and empathy she provided so selflessly and given her nothing. And then he'd compounded his mistakes by kissing her. Any one of her brothers would probably be happy to give him the punch in the jaw he richly deserved.

He shoved open the swinging door to the break room, stepped inside—and there she was. Terry turned from the coffeepot, mug in her hand, her cheeks brightening at the sight of him. It was too late to retreat now. Maybe, if his head would just stop pounding so much, he could try to make amends.

"Jake—Dr. Landsdowne." She gestured toward the cup. "Harriet said I could help myself to coffee. I mean—"

"It's okay, Terry." He managed a smile. "So far, the budget axe hasn't fallen on our coffee fund. Help yourself. Did you and Jeff bring the nursing home patient in?"

"Our last run of the shift." She took a sip of the coffee. "I have to confess, this is better than the coffee we've been making at the clinic. My mother took one taste and insisted she's bringing in a new coffeemaker. And some decent coffee."

"It certainly couldn't hurt." He gulped, feeling a touch of relief the instant the hot liquid hit. "Is she at the clinic today?"

Terry nodded. "She was also taking some more books for Manuela. That kid must be a speed reader, and in a second language, no less."

"She's a bright girl." He needed to say something to her about the previous day, but his brain seemed fogged. "Listen, Terry, about yesterday—"

"Please, don't." Anything that had seemed relaxed about her manner toward him vanished in an instant. "It's fine. Really. It's forgotten."

She thought he was talking about that kiss. Oddly enough, that was the one thing that had happened between them that he didn't regret.

"I just wanted you to know I think you're a fine paramedic. I've been saying all the wrong things about that lately. We've worked together long enough that I don't doubt your skill or your devotion."

She flushed, but this time he thought it was with pleasure. "Thank you. I'm sure you'll still have to put me in my place from time to time."

He managed a smile, but the buzzing in his head was so loud he didn't think he could say a word. He put the mug down, rocking it so badly that coffee sloshed onto the table.

"Jake?" Terry grasped his arm, her grip firm. "You're sick." She put her hand on his cheek and then jerked it away. "You're burning up. You shouldn't be working in this condition. Why didn't you say anything?"

"It's nothing." It wasn't nothing. He knew what it was, but no one else must know.

"You have a fever. You can't treat patients. I'll call Harriet."

"No!" He grabbed her hand. "Don't. You're right. I shouldn't be here. I'll go home."

"Let her check you out."

He tightened his grip, his head spinning. "Nobody can know. I have to get home. My meds are there. But nobody can know." He tried to push himself erect, but the walls were wavering oddly. "I'll go."

Terry slid his arm across her shoulders, bracing his body with hers, and he was surprised at the strength of her. "Not by yourself," she said firmly. "I'll drive your car for you."

He tried to concentrate. "You can't leave work—"

"My shift is over. Jeff will take the rig back to the firehouse."

He couldn't do this. He couldn't let Terry, of all people, see how weak he was. Panic flooded through him, giving the momentary illusion of strength. He couldn't let anyone know. He had to pull it together long enough to get to his car, get home.

"You don't have to drive me." He tried to put some energy into the words. She'd never release him if she guessed how bad he was.

"I'm not letting you get behind the wheel of a car in this condition, so get used to the idea. If you don't want me to take you, fine." He heard the hurt in her voice. "Just give me the name of someone else I can call for you."

He couldn't. That was the barren truth. There was no one else in Suffolk that he could call to help him.

He closed his eyes for a moment. *Please. Help me.* When he opened them, he still felt like passing out. And Terry still watched him with anxiety clouding those clear green eyes.

Maybe God wasn't answering him. Or maybe that's why Terry was here at just this moment.

"All right," he muttered, trying to shrug out of his lab coat.

Terry moved quickly, pulling it off and hanging it on one of the hooks. He picked up the phone, dialing Harriet.

"I think I'm coming down with a cold." He rushed the words out. "Can you hold the fort if I go home early?"

"Of course." Her cool, professional tone didn't allow her to sound pleased. "Do you want me to have a look at you?"

"No. Thanks. I'll be fine." He clicked off. She'd think him rude, but that was better than having her know the truth.

No, it seemed that Terry was the one person destined to know the truth about him. Well, if she'd ever nursed a secret longing to see him at his worst, at his weakest, she was certainly getting her chance today.

Terry wanted to turn around a half-dozen times during the drive to Jake's condo and take him straight back to the E.R. If he were anyone else, she'd have continued to try and get him to see a doctor. But Jake was the doc, and whatever was going on, it was obviously familiar to him. Supposedly he knew how to handle it. Still, she wasn't about to leave him alone until she was sure he'd be all right, whether he liked it or not.

Not was most probably the answer to that. Well, she'd deal with it when the time came.

The address he'd given her was in a condo development down near the river—town houses, for the most part, that had been sold to young families and a few single young professionals. She frowned, weaving her way through the older residential streets that surrounded it. Funny that she hadn't even thought about where Jake lived. She only associated him with the hospital and the clinic.

She glanced at him. He'd surprised her by managing to walk out of the hospital without hanging on to her, but how was she going to get him into the house? He leaned back against the headrest, eyes closed, his skin clammy and gray.

"We're almost there. What number did you say it was?"

He roused himself to open his eyes. "It's 1142. In the next block, the end unit on the right."

The buildings had brick facing on the lower level with white siding on the second floors. Jake's door was a glossy burgundy, and rosebushes, still putting out a few blossoms, flanked a front porch just large enough for two wicker chairs. The geraniums in hanging pots surprised her—she wouldn't have expected him to take an interest in plant care. But maybe the condos had a gardener to deal with such chores.

She mentally measured the distance from curb to front door. "Is there a way to get closer? A back entrance?" She was used to hauling limp bodies, but moving Jake without help would be a chore.

"No." He sat up straighter. "I can manage. Just let me off here."

"Right. And watch you collapse on the sidewalk."

She slid out of the car, shaking her head. Was it just Jake? No, probably her brothers would be just as irritated at showing weakness in front of her.

She reached the passenger door as he opened it. As she suspected, he had an unpleasant surprise when he tried to get out. It took a couple of uncomfortable, sweating moments before he was standing on the walk, leaning on her, both of them breathing hard.

She took a firm grip on his arm, slung across her shoulder, and gripped his waist with her other arm. "Okay. Let's just take it slow."

"Don't have to talk to me as if I'm one of your patients," he muttered.

"Wouldn't dream of it." She piloted him toward the door, his weight seeming to get heavier with each step. "But I am used to dealing with people who don't know what's good for them."

His only response to that was a grunt. He was probably trying as hard as she was just to stay upright.

Finally they reached the porch. She gave a sigh of relief and propped him against one of the chairs. "Key?"

He fumbled in his pocket and drew out a key ring. "I can do—" The keys slid through his fingers and bounced, jingling, on the brick porch.

"Please," she said. "You can't even hold them, let alone get the key in the lock. If any of your neighbors are watching, they're probably sure you're drunk."

His mouth twitched, as if in the beginning of a smile. "'Good people, we are not drunk, as you might suppose,'" he quoted.

It startled her to hear Peter's words on the day of Pentecost coming from Jake's mouth. She wouldn't have supposed he knew the Bible that well.

That was certainly a sanctimonious thought. *Sorry, Father.*

"Well, it's not nine o'clock in the morning, either." She swung the door open. "Come on, let's get you inside."

She piloted him in, spotted a comfortable-looking black leather sofa, and steered him to it. He slid onto it and tilted his head back, breathing heavily. Worry edged along her nerves. Was she doing the right thing by not calling Harriet?

"Tell me where your meds are, and I'll get them," she said abruptly, hating the feeling of being kept in the dark, the possibility of making a mistake because of his stubbornness.

He shook his head slowly, rolling it back and forth against the leather. "I can manage. You can leave—"

"No way. Look, Jake, I've only gone along with you this far because you're a doctor and I hope you know what you're doing. But either you let me give you the meds right now, or I'm calling Dr. Getz."

His glare was a feeble effort, and he must have realized that. He closed his eyes. "Upstairs medicine cabinet. Chloroquinine."

Chloroquinine. So that was it. Malaria. He'd obviously contracted it in Africa and was having a relapse.

She frowned. "I don't know much about malaria, but isn't there a drug that prevents relapses?"

He nodded. "But only if you're fortunate enough to tolerate it. Are you going?"

"Right."

She went quickly up the staircase, running her hand along the satiny finish of the railing. The stairway was lined with framed color photos of African scenes, obviously personal to Jake. She shot a quick glance across what she could see of the living area. No family pictures. His relationship, or lack of one, with his family wasn't any of her business.

The bathroom was black-and-white tile with an Art Deco feel. She glanced quickly through the shelves of the medicine cabinet. The chloroquinine was the only prescription med there. She grabbed it, filled the bathroom cup with water and hurried back down, mind busy with the implications of Jake's illness.

He didn't want anyone to know, that much was clear. Did that mean he hadn't told anyone from the hospital when they'd hired him?

When she reached Jake, he'd slid down to a lying position on the sofa, head against the wide arm. She slipped her hand under his head to lift it, seeing the muscles of his neck work as he swallowed the pill.

"Okay," he muttered. "You can—"

"If you tell me to leave again, I might hit you," she warned.

The ghost of a smile flickered on his lips. "I'm too weak to fight back."

"I'll get a blanket and pillow for you." She straightened, but as she did, he caught her hand. His felt hot and dry. "What is it? Do you want something else?"

He shook his head slowly, as if even that took an effort. "Just thinking," he murmured. "If you wanted something to use against me, you have it now."

"Why, for goodness' sake? You're sick. That's not criminal. Unless you didn't tell them when they hired you—" She hated to think that.

"Not that." His voice faded to a whisper. "Just failure. Failure." He slid into sleep.

Chapter Ten

"Thanks, Seth. And tell Mom thanks, too." Terry kept her voice low as she closed the door of Jake's condo behind her brother.

She probably didn't need to be so careful. Jake had been asleep for three solid hours, and he didn't look as if anything short of a thunderclap would disturb him.

Her mother had sent Seth over to deliver a couple of quarts of homemade chicken soup—her remedy for everything from the sniffles to a broken heart. She hadn't told Mom what was wrong with Jake, but surely chicken soup couldn't hurt.

She paused on her way to the kitchen to put her hand on Jake's forehead. She didn't need a thermometer to tell her he was still burning with fever. So how long did she take responsibility for him without calling in another doctor?

She could call Harriet. They were friends—surely she could ask for advice, couldn't she?

But she knew the answer to that. Jake didn't want Harriet to know. He'd made that very clear.

Please, Father, guide me. I'm not sure what to do, and I don't want to make a mistake.

That seemed to be her theme song for the past few years. I don't want to make a mistake.

Trying to push away the sensation of helplessness, she took the soup to the kitchen. After a moment's hesitation, she rummaged through the cabinets until she found a saucepan and dumped a quart of chicken soup into it. Maybe by the time it had heated, Jake would be stirring.

She put the soup on low and went back to the living room, drawn to check on him again, even though it seemed unlikely that anything would have changed in the past three minutes. She settled into the overstuffed leather chair opposite the couch, studying Jake's face.

Pale, with the faintest dark stubble beginning to show. The sharp lines of his features seemed less aggressive in sleep, his mouth softer. His head turned a little, as if he searched for a cooler spot on the pillow.

But even as she thought that, a shiver went through him. She got up quickly, grabbing the extra blanket she'd found in the linen closet. Chills and fever. She'd spent a few minutes on Jake's computer, trying to become an instant expert on malaria. He had the fever, now he was going to battle the chills.

She tucked the blanket around him. "It's okay, Jake. I know you're cold."

His eyes struggled to open, so dark the blue was almost midnight. He frowned at her, as if trying to identify who she was and why she was here.

"Terry. What—" The words were interrupted by a spasm of chills that set his teeth chattering.

"It's okay," she said again. "You took your pills about

two hours ago, and you've been asleep. Is there anything else I can do to make you more comfortable?"

A shudder shook him. "Another blanket."

"Right." She ran up the stairs, pulled the comforter off his bed, and hurried back down again. *Lord, please let me be doing the right thing.*

She tossed the comforter over him, tucking it around his body. He nodded, as if to thank her.

"My mother sent over some chicken soup. I have it warm on the stove. Do you think you could eat some?"

Weak as he was, he managed a glare. "You told her."

"Just that you're sick, not what the problem is. She always figures chicken soup couldn't hurt. How about it?"

He nodded. "Worth a try." The words were interrupted by another round of teeth-rattling chills.

It hurt to watch him. She hurried out to the kitchen and ladled soup into a mug. It might be easier for him to sip it than to try and use a spoon, and he probably wouldn't let her feed him. Everyone said doctors were the worst patients.

She knelt next to him and held the mug to his lips. "Just try a sip," she coaxed.

He managed to get a few mouthfuls down before the next chill hit. Was it wishful thinking, or were the chills a little less violent?

"Better now," he murmured. His eyes closed, his lashes dark against his pallor.

"That's quite a souvenir you brought back from Africa." She set the mug on the lamp table, close at hand. "Does this happen often?"

A frown set three sharp vertical lines between his brows. "I thought I'd had the last episode." His eyes snapped open. "Dr. Getz knows about it, if that's what you're wondering."

There wasn't much she could say in answer to that, since she had been wondering. "But you don't want anyone else to know."

"I don't want to give the rumor factory any fresh ammunition. My position at the hospital is precarious enough already." His mouth set stubbornly.

At least he wasn't shaking any longer. She offered him the mug. He took it and downed about half of it before slumping back against the pillows again, exhausted.

"You know your business best, I guess. But I think most people would find your work in Africa impressive, especially when it came at such a price."

He focused on her, frowning. "You mean the malaria?"

"Well, that, too. But I was thinking about giving up your residency, the plans you'd made for your future—"

His mouth twisted. "You and Getz, you're the same. Attributing noble motives to me. Believe me, it wasn't all that noble. I went to the mission field because no one else wanted me."

She could only stare at him. "But your residency—"

"I was allowed to resign, allowed to cover it up with talk of health problems."

"I didn't know."

His head moved restlessly again. "The truth was that after Meredith's death I couldn't cope. I started second-guessing myself. I was no good to anyone. If I hadn't resigned, they'd have dropped me from the program." He bit the words off as if they tasted vile.

"I'm sorry." Jake always seemed so sure of himself. She'd have expected him to ignore everyone else's opinion, but maybe his own sense of guilt had whispered that they were right. "If you didn't want to go to the mission, surely there were other options. Your father must have so many connections."

His jaw clenched. "Connections? Yes, he has those. But he wouldn't use them. He wouldn't even recommend me when people he knew called him, thinking they'd give me a chance because I was his son."

"I don't understand. Surely he wanted to help you." Her parents would sacrifice anything to help one of their own.

"I'd failed. That reflected on him." He said the words evenly, but she could hear the pain he suppressed. "I didn't have what it took, letting myself get emotionally involved, showing weakness. He cut me off, as if he'd never had a son."

She tried to absorb it, to understand it, but she couldn't. She could never understand someone who'd behave that way to his own child.

"I'm sorry." Her hand closed over his, feeling the tension that gripped him. "I don't know what to say."

"You want to make it better?" A faint thread of mockery traced the words. "No one can make this better. All I can do is make it on my own. That's why I went to Somalia. Because they'd take me, and because I knew I'd be so busy there that I wouldn't have time to think."

"You did good work there. No matter why you went, you can't lose sight of the good you did."

He nodded slowly, meeting her gaze, his very serious. "In the midst of all that pain and turmoil, I met people who carried their own center of peace with them. It was a life-changing experience to work with them. For the first time, I took my focus off myself and turned my life over to God."

"I'm glad," she said simply, her throat tight with unshed tears.

His head moved restlessly on the pillow. "I thought I was doing what God wanted, but then the malaria hit, and they sent me home. Is that what God had planned for me, Terry? If you have an answer, give it to me, because I don't understand."

"If I had all the answers, I wouldn't struggle every day with my own doubts and fears. But I know one thing—God has the answers for you. You have to stop telling yourself you failed. Malaria is an illness, not a personal weakness."

He shook his head. His eyes closed, as if he'd talked himself into exhaustion. She stayed where she was, kneeling next to him, holding his hand, as he drifted into sleep.

He needs so much to do good work, Father. Please, let him see that he's punishing himself unnecessarily. Let him find his path.

Because if he didn't—she didn't want to think about what might become of Jake if he lost this position. So she'd keep his secret, and she'd do her best to help him.

And if her own heart got bruised in the process? Well, she'd just have to deal with that as best she could.

Jake struggled awake. Why was he on the sofa? He shoved away the blankets that muffled him, and memory came flooding back. He put his hand to his head, feeling the perspiration that streaked his hair.

Another relapse, just when he'd thought he was past all that. He gritted his teeth and pushed to an upright position. He was as weak as a newborn kitten, but at least the fever was gone. By morning, he'd be able to go back to work as if nothing had happened.

China clinked in the kitchen, reminding him that he had bigger problems than going back to work in the morning. Terry. He hadn't dreamed it. Terry had brought him home, had stayed with him. He had a hazy memory of her strong, capable hands tucking blankets around him.

He'd depended on her. Worse, he'd talked to her, spilling out things he'd never told a living soul. He'd trusted her with his future.

Terry was trustworthy. The thought had a feel of bedrock truth about it. Still, how reliable was his judgment? He'd certainly made a string of mistakes when it came to dealing with the emotional side of his life.

He heard her light step, and Terry came quickly through the doorway to the kitchen. She checked a moment at the sight of him sitting up and then came toward him.

"You may live after all." Her palm was cool against his forehead. "The fever's gone."

"That seems to be the pattern." He tried to keep his tone light. "Headache, fever, chills and eventually I sleep it off."

She eyed him critically. "But you still look as if a light breeze would knock you over. Could you manage some soup and toast?"

"You don't need to nurse me, Terry. I'm over the worst of it." And he didn't want to depend on her any longer. The longer she stayed, the greater the risk he'd do or say something he'd regret.

Her smile flashed, lighting her face. "I'm a paramedic, remember? You just get emergency care from me."

"No TLC?" Keep it light. They were colleagues, nothing more.

"No, but my mother would never forgive me if I left without feeding you again. That's her answer to life's problems—lots of love and a good meal."

"Sounds like a pretty good recipe to me." He leaned back, knowing if he tried to get up he'd fall on his face. "Okay, soup and toast, but only if you have some, too." He glanced toward the window. Dark outside, and Terry had turned on the lamps. "You must have missed your supper."

"No problem." She turned back to the kitchen. "You get used to eating at odd times when you work shifts."

This might be one of the coziest meals of his life, sitting side by side with Terry on the couch, plates on the coffee table, eating soup and buttered toast. Finally he leaned back, tired but with the relieved conviction that this relapse was over. Maybe the last one. Optimism buoyed him. He'd escaped again, and no one but Terry knew.

His gaze rested on her as she scooped up the last spoonful of soup. Her hair was ruffled, and any makeup she might have worn had long since vanished. The paramedic khaki pants and navy shirt looked as if they'd been slept in. She was the best thing he'd seen in a long time.

"Terry."

She turned her head, smiling at him. "What?"

"Just—thanks." It seemed a small return.

She shrugged, looking embarrassed. "Mom supplied the chicken soup."

"Not just for the food. For everything. I seem to recall being pretty rude to you when you were trying to help me."

Her eyebrows lifted. "Would it surprise you to learn that patients are often rude to paramedics?"

"No. But I'm not just a patient."

She was perched on the edge of the sofa, and he wanted her closer. He circled her wrist with his fingers, feeling her pulse accelerate at his touch.

"They do say doctors make the worst patients." The words came out with a breathless quality.

"We do. All the more reason for me to apologize." He leaned toward her, his native caution warring with the longing he felt to hold her close.

"Forget it." Her voice had gone soft, and she turned more fully toward him. "Call it professional courtesy, or—"

The rest of the words were lost when his lips found hers. He shouldn't. But she was here. He cared for her. Her arms slid around him, her lips soft against his, and a wave of tenderness swept through him. He wanted to hold her, to go on holding her, to feel her warmth and caring and know that it was for him.

She drew back finally, a smile trembling on her lips. "I thought we weren't going to do that again." The words were a bare whisper, for his ears only.

"I don't think I promised that, did I?" He slid his arm around her, drawing her close so that her head rested on his shoulder. "I'm glad you're here, Terry. Glad you were the one in the break room when I walked in today."

"Me, too." Her head moved slightly against his shoulder. "I do think you shouldn't worry so much about people knowing, though. They'd consider malaria a badge of honor after the work you did."

"Maybe, but I can't afford to take the risk. And I'm not sure I did anything that admirable."

"Jake—"

He shook his head. He didn't want her looking at him as if he'd done something heroic. "Just let it go. Please."

Concern for him darkened her eyes. "What is it? Were you trying to make up for Meredith's death by saving other people?"

The question hit him right in the gut. That was exactly what he'd been trying to do in Somalia. His mouth twisted.

"If it was, I failed. I turned into a patient myself instead of saving others. Maybe God was telling me that nothing I did was enough to make up for what I didn't do for Meredith."

"Jake, you can't think that. You did good work there, and you're doing good work now. You can't blame yourself—"

"Yes. I can." He shook his head, hating the pity he saw in her face. "Don't. This is something you can't make better. Nobody can."

He'd made a mistake, letting Terry get so close, letting her pity him. His father had been right about him. He'd let emotions cloud his judgment again. He should have realized he didn't have anything to offer Terry.

There wasn't a future for their relationship, but he couldn't push her away. Selfish, but he just couldn't do it.

"Are you sure they're going to like ham and scalloped potatoes?" Terry glanced across the church kitchen at her mother, who was putting the final touches to an immense tossed salad. Gelatin salads already chilled in the refrigerator.

"I asked Manuela, and she said that would be great." Her mother smiled. "Let's face it, Terry. We couldn't have put together a meal of Mexican food they'd even recognize."

"I guess you're right."

Inviting people from the migrant camps to the church for a home-cooked meal had been Mom's idea, and she'd marshaled her troops like a general. Volunteers had worked through the afternoon, and even now were setting the tables in Fellowship Hall. The aroma of baked ham was nearly irresistible.

"I invited Jake." Mom wedged the last salad into the refrigerator. "Do you think he'll come?"

"I'm not sure," she hedged. "He might not be able to get away from the hospital in time."

In fact, she wasn't sure of a lot about Jake right now, even though her lips curved into an automatic smile at the thought of him. She had it bad, all right. And she just didn't know if he felt the same.

He'd regretted confiding so much in her the night he'd been sick. She was convinced of that. If she tried to bring up the subject, he'd tense, so she'd stopped trying.

Still, he seemed to want to spend time with her. They'd even gone out on what she supposed was their first official date—dinner out after closing the clinic down the previous night. He'd steered the conversation away from anything personal, but his good-night kiss certainly hadn't been impersonal.

She turned to check the status of the scalloped potato casseroles, hoping Mom would think her cheeks were pink from the oven's heat. She didn't want to talk about Jake, because she couldn't be sure there was anything in their relationship.

She probably shouldn't have said what she had about

his motives, and yet it seemed so clear to her. How many lives did he think he had to save to make up for failing Meredith? He'd never think he'd done enough. And as long as he couldn't forgive himself, he couldn't accept God's forgiveness.

She closed the oven door. Maybe Brendan had an answer for that one. She didn't.

Mom folded a tea towel neatly on the rack. "Speaking of Manuela, Brendan told me he tried to speak to Matthew Dixon, but ended up talking to Andy instead. Andy promised to do what he could to see that the Ortiz family stays through the apple harvest, at least."

"I wish he'd hurry up with it. School started yesterday, but none of the migrant children from the Dixon camp went. I know Manuela is wild to go."

If the Ortiz family left in another week, they might never see Manuela again. The family would follow the harvest, and who knew what would happen to them then? Her heart hurt at the thought of never seeing Manuela again.

"I know." Mom's smooth brow wrinkled. "Your father and I have been talking about it. If there's no other way to help them, we'd like to offer to have Manuela stay with us and go to school. I don't know how her family would react, or what the legalities would be, but we'd like to try."

"You'd be willing to do that?" Silly question, really. Mom was noted for taking in strays. Dad grumbled sometimes, but he was secretly proud of her open heart.

"Of course." Her mother smiled. "We're used to having those bedrooms filled. In fact, we might be getting a full house for a while. I had a letter yesterday from your cousin Fiona. She'd like to come to see us."

"Fiona?" For a moment she was too stunned to say more. "But—Dad hasn't had any contact with her father in thirty years."

The breach between her husband and his younger brother was a grief to Mom, Terry knew. She'd struggled to maintain some contact, even though Michael Flanagan had settled in California years ago. Terry knew her cousins existed, but she'd never even met them.

"All the more reason why we should welcome Michael's daughter to our home," her mother said tartly. "It's time to put this foolishness behind us."

"Does Dad think so?"

"Not yet. But I'm working on him." She glanced through the pass-through window to Fellowship Hall. "Look, Jake did come."

Everything else slid to the back of Terry's mind as she saw Jake's tall figure sauntering toward them, pausing to greet the workers who'd finished setting the tables and now sat in a circle, chatting.

He reached them, his smile deepening as he looked at Terry. "Hi, Terry. Siobhan. What's for supper?"

"Can't you smell it? Baked ham."

"And you're just in time," her mother said. She glanced at the clock over the range. "Goodness, look at the clock. The food's about ready. They should be here by now. Brendan sent the bus for them ages ago."

Jake frowned. "You know, it would be like the crew chief to keep them working late tonight, just out of spite. I think I'll call Andy Dixon and see if he knows what's going on." He pulled out his cell phone and flipped it open.

It felt good to know Jake was on her side in this, at

least. She studied him as he talked, liking the strength in his face, the determination in his jaw. Funny, he no longer seemed to have that superior look she'd told herself she disliked so much. Or maybe he hadn't changed, but her way of looking at him had.

He hung up after several minutes, shaking his head. "That's exactly what happened. Andy intervened, and they're getting on the bus now."

"Thank goodness you thought of calling." Siobhan beamed at him. "Otherwise we'd have been sitting here letting the food dry out." She clapped her hands to get the attention of her helpers. "They're on their way, ladies. Let's get the ham sliced and the biscuits baked."

In a moment the kitchen was a hive of activity, and Terry was swept into it, relegated to putting salads out on the long serving table. By the time she had a chance to look up, their guests were filing into Fellowship Hall, a little quiet and uncomfortable at first, but relaxing when they saw familiar faces from the clinic.

In the bustle of serving, she lost track of Jake, but when things calmed down, she scanned the room, finding him in the corner, deep in conversation with Andy. They certainly owed Andy a vote of thanks for intervening in the crew chief's troublemaking. Now, if he'd done as he promised and talked to his father about having the Ortiz family stay, they'd really owe him.

She pulled off the apron her mother had insisted she wear over her khaki slacks and crossed the room to them. Andy's pleasant face broke into a smile when he saw her.

"Well, do I get an extra slice of pie for my efforts?"

"As much as you can eat. We can't thank you enough."

He shrugged. "I'm just glad Jake called. I'm afraid

it was a case of the crew chief trying to enforce his authority at your expense."

"It worked out," Jake said. "That's the important thing."

"What about our other problem?" It certainly couldn't hurt to prod Andy a little. "Have you talked to your father about letting the Ortiz family stay through the apple harvest?"

Andy's smile disappeared, and she knew what he was going to say before the words were out. "I'm sorry, Terry. I tried, but Dad has been impossible lately. As soon as I got the words out, he started ranting about do-gooders trying to interfere with how he runs his own farm."

"But didn't you explain that we're only trying to help Manuela have a chance at some stable schooling?" She tried to ignore the frown Jake was directing at her, the one that told her not to make waves.

"Honestly, Terry, it wouldn't have done any good to keep pushing him then. I'll try to bring it up again, I promise."

"Thank you," Jake said quickly. "That's all we can ask."

Well, that might be all Jake wanted to ask, but it wasn't enough for her. She'd give Andy another day or two to come through for them, but if that didn't work, she'd see Matthew Dixon herself, no matter how much Jake disapproved.

Chapter Eleven

Jake didn't like to admit what it said about his feelings that he was lingering near the emergency room admissions desk just because he knew Terry's unit was coming in with a nursing home transfer. The admissions clerk would handle sending the patient to the lab for tests. There was no reason for the Director of Emergency Services to be here, except that he wanted to see Terry's bright smile.

He pulled a chart from the rack and scanned it. Busywork, the rational side of his mind mocked him. You're trying to look busy so no one will know you're waiting here for Terry, like a high-school kid lingering near his sweetheart's locker.

Not a sweetheart, he assured himself. He didn't have a sophomoric crush on Terry. He enjoyed her company. That didn't have to mean anything serious for either of them.

For the first time in a long while, he had a sense of cautious optimism about the future. The thought startled him. He felt as if he were taking the first steps toward a normal life, and he couldn't deny that Terry had something to do with that.

Terry, and the mix of attraction, affection and caring he felt at just the sight of her as she and her partner moved a patient on a gurney toward the glass doors. Terry leaned over the gurney as she pushed, her face lit with that warm, caring smile, assuring her patient that everything was all right.

Even though he was prepared for it, the rush of pure pleasure he felt as she came toward him startled him with its strength. He tried to put on his usual professional demeanor as they neared.

"Good morning. Do you have a patient for us?" He'd like to believe Terry's smile was a bit warmer when it was aimed at him.

"Good morning, Dr. Landsdowne." Her tone was perfectly sedate, as if he hadn't kissed her good night at her door the previous night when he'd driven her home after the supper at church. "Mr. Atkins is just scheduled for some routine blood work, that's all."

"I'll check him in," Terry's partner offered. "No problem." He shoved the gurney over to the admissions clerk.

Just how much did Terry's partner know about them? He shoved that thought to the back of his mind. There wasn't really anything to know, was there?

"I hope your mother is taking it easy today, after everything she did yesterday to put on that dinner. Will you be having leftover ham for the rest of the week?"

"Mom doesn't know the meaning of taking it easy. And you don't have to worry about the food—she packaged up all the leftovers and took them out to the migrant camp."

"It was a big success—" The buzz of his beeper cut off his words. He checked it and frowned. "Dr. Getz. Excuse me."

He moved quickly to the phone on the desk and dialed the chief of staff's extension. The clerk was at the far end of the counter, dealing with the patient's paperwork. No one but Terry was close enough to hear. Maybe his optimism about the way things were going was misplaced. Why did the chief want him?

"Landsdowne, I'm glad I caught you." At least Getz didn't sound as if he'd called with a complaint. "Your father is here to see you. You can use my office to talk. Just come right up." He clicked off, leaving Jake staring at the phone.

Jake fumbled the receiver back on the phone, turning toward Terry without even thinking about the instant need to confide in her. "He says my father is here to see me."

Her gaze rested on his face. "Do you want to see him?"

"No!" The response was automatic. "Why would I? He's the one who cut me off." He reached for the phone. "I'll tell Getz to say I'm not available."

She stopped the movement of his hand with hers. "Don't, Jake. You don't want to put Dr. Getz in the middle of your quarrel with your father."

"It's not a quarrel." But she had a point. He shouldn't involve the chief of staff in a personal matter. It seemed his father had already done that.

"Still—"

"I know." He clasped her hand, grateful that she was

here. "You're right. I'll have to speak to my father myself and make it clear there's nothing else to say."

Her eyebrows lifted. "Are you sure? I mean, he wouldn't be here if he didn't want to talk to you. His coming here must mean his attitude toward you has changed."

"You don't know my father. Once he's made up his mind, nothing changes it."

"He said things in anger. Everyone does that." She leaned toward him, intent in her desire to make things better. That was Terry, always trying to make things better.

"You're seeing the world through your family's rose-colored glasses." He thought perhaps a bit enviously of Joe Flanagan's obvious pride in his children, of Siobhan's overflowing love. "My family isn't like yours."

"Maybe so, but you still have to see him. You know that." Her hand clasped his persuasively. "If you don't hear him out, someday you'll regret it. Maybe not now, but someday. You don't want that hanging on your conscience."

"Your conscience is tenderer than mine." He smiled wryly. "But you're probably right. I have to see him. And he can't say anything that will matter to me any longer, in any event."

He hoped. Still, he didn't really have a choice, did he? Terry was right. He had to do this.

"Ready to head back?" Jeff paused at the corner of the desk, lifting his eyebrows at her. His expression suggested that he knew exactly why she lingered there and was trying to imply that he didn't.

She glanced at her watch. "As long as we don't have

any calls, why don't we just wait for Mr. Atkins to be ready to go back?"

"Sure, save us a trip. Want to get some lunch?"

"I'm not hungry right now. You go ahead." Did he buy that? Well, it didn't matter. Jeff might suspect, but he wouldn't gossip.

He nodded and ambled down the pale green corridor toward the hospital cafeteria.

She shouldn't hang around here, waiting for Jake to come back. That implied that she thought he should tell her what was going on with his father.

She bent over the counter, concentrating on filling out the run sheet. Routine, nothing but routine. It didn't keep her from thinking about Jake.

Lord, please be with Jake right now. His relationship with his father is beyond my understanding, but You know all about it. Jake has given his life to You. Please guide him now.

She didn't know what else to pray for. There was nothing simple or easy to understand about Jake, or about her feelings for him, for that matter. She leaned against the counter, gaze absently fixed on the bowl of yellow chrysanthemums that decorated it.

Yellow mums for fall. The season was moving on. Jake had been in Suffolk for a month now. Did he feel that he was fitting in, finding a home here? Or did he carry that restless, rootless feeling inside him?

She had to face facts. Until he'd resolved his feelings about failing Meredith, Jake wouldn't be free to love anyone else. Not that she was thinking about love in connection with him. She backed away from that quickly.

If she were thinking that—her mind drifted to her

brothers, all happily married now. To her parents. There were plenty of examples of God-centered, solid, happy marriages in her family. That was what she wanted for herself. She wouldn't make the mistake of letting herself fall in love with someone who couldn't make that kind of commitment.

She was still standing there, frowning at the run sheet as if it held the secret of the universe, when the elevator doors swished open. Jake stalked out, and one look at his face told her the meeting with his father hadn't gone well.

"Jake—"

He shot a glance toward the receptionist, shook his head and took her arm. "Let's go in the lounge." He piloted her quickly toward the staff lounge, and she could feel the depth of his anger through the taut fingers that gripped her elbow.

As soon as the door closed behind them, Jake released her. He stalked across the room, looking as if he'd like to punch his fist into the wall, then turned back toward her.

"Tell me what happened."

Jake had to talk to someone, or he was going to explode. She already knew about his situation with his father. If he talked to her about it, it would only be because she was the one person who knew. Nothing more.

He turned away, planting both fists on the table, looking down. Tension was written in every line of his body. He looked as if he'd fly apart at any moment.

"Please, Jake," she said softly. "Talk to me. What did he say?"

He straightened, running his hand through his hair as if that would help him put his thoughts together.

"Nothing I shouldn't have expected." He shook his head. "Oh, it started out well enough. After all, the fact that he was here showed he'd at least been interested enough to keep tabs on where I am."

"That's good, isn't it?" There was nothing in that to account for the anger that radiated from Jake in waves.

His mouth twisted. "You'd think so. Sounds like something any father might do. But he went a bit further. He got in touch with Getz and asked him if he found my work satisfactory." He sounded as if he were quoting. "Satisfactory! As if that's the best that could be expected from me."

"Whatever your father's motives, I'm sure Dr. Getz gave a good report about you." She was feeling her way, not sure what would ease the pain she sensed beneath the anger. Her heart hurt for him.

"Yes. He did. That's why my father came to see me." His hands flexed, then drew tight, the knuckles white. "Since my work has been satisfactory, he's decided to give me another chance. According to him, I'm wasting my talent here. I'm to give up my work, go back to Boston and take up the neurosurgery residency he's managed to wangle for me."

Go back to Boston. For a moment she faced the prospect of life without Jake. It looked bleak. She took a breath. This wasn't about her. It was about Jake.

"That's what you've always wanted, isn't it?"

"Yes. No, I'm not sure anymore what I want." He pressed his knuckles against his forehead. "One thing I know—I don't want my father telling me what to do. Not anymore."

"Jake—" This is about Jake, remember? Not about

you. "Look, it sounds as if he went about talking to you all wrong, but maybe you should still think about it. Don't throw away an opportunity because you're angry with him."

"That's not it." He tried, and failed, to smile, and then came quickly back across the room to clasp her hands in his. "I don't know whether neurosurgery is what I want anymore, but even if it is, I don't think I'm willing to pay the price my father asks." His fingers tightened on hers, robbing her of the ability to breathe. "Thank you, Terry. For caring."

Caring. Her heart was too full to speak, and she couldn't kid herself any longer. What she felt for Jake wasn't caring, or friendship, or sympathy. It was love.

She was in love with him, whether there was any future in that or not.

Terry was supposed to be on her way to the clinic, but no one needed to know that she planned to make a stop first. She turned down the lane that led to the Dixon farmhouse. She could only hope she'd find Matthew Dixon at home, preferably alone.

Depending on Andy to intercede with his father didn't seem to be getting them anywhere. Each day that passed made it more difficult for Manuela to start school. She hadn't been much help to Jake the previous day, but maybe she could accomplish something for Manuela if she could talk to Mr. Dixon.

He might think of her as Joe Flanagan's little girl, but he respected her father. Maybe he'd listen to her when he wouldn't listen to his son. Fathers and sons sometimes didn't respect each other's opinions—she only had to look at Jake's relationship with his father to see that.

Her heart clenched for him. Was Jake giving up something he'd regret later? That was what she feared. It would break her heart if he left, but if he stayed and felt he'd settled for second best, that would be worse.

She couldn't help but wonder if that interview with his father was as bad as Jake felt. Had his father really intended to denigrate Jake's accomplishments, or was Jake reading something into it out of his past pain? She didn't know, and she probably never would.

She pulled to a stop in front of the farmhouse. She'd been so preoccupied with thoughts of Jake that she hadn't rehearsed what she was going to say to Mr. Dixon. Well, maybe that was just as well.

Please, Lord. I believe I'm doing Your will in this. So please, speak through me.

She didn't see Andy's car anywhere. Maybe she'd be fortunate enough to find him out. Andy's protectiveness toward his father might be admirable, but in this case, she could do without it.

She went quickly to the screen door and rapped, the weathered door rattling under her assault. She paused for a moment, hand on that door. Had someone called out?

"Come in." The voice, sounding querulous, came from upstairs. "Come here and help me."

Nobody ever had to say "help me" twice to her. Terry yanked open the screen door and hurried across the hall and up the stairs. "Mr. Dixon? Are you all right?"

"In here." Dixon stood in the doorway of a bedroom, barefoot, his white hair ruffled. "Who are you?"

"Terry Flanagan, Mr. Dixon." He looked upset, but not ill. "You remember me. Joe Flanagan's girl."

"'Course I remember you." His voice was testy. "Just can't see you without my glasses, that's all. Fool boy is supposed to leave them on the nightstand so I can find them, and he didn't. Can't even get my shoes on without them."

"Suppose I have a look around for them?" She moved past him into the bedroom. Dark, heavy furniture, the relics of an earlier age. Light-blocking shades were pulled down at the windows, making the interior of the room cavelike.

No wonder he couldn't find his glasses. She practically had to grope her way across the room to the window in order to flip up the shades, letting sunlight flood the room. Mr. Dixon blinked, like an owl exposed to the light.

"Those glasses have to be here somewhere. Use your eyes, girl. Find them." His bark sounded more assured now.

"Yes, sir." The glasses were probably right on the nightstand where Andy was supposed to leave them. But she checked the nightstand and then the floor around it without finding them.

"Well, where are they?"

Dixon took a step toward her, his hand out in front of him as if feeling for any obstacles, and she realized how little he could see without his glasses. A wave of pity swept through her. How terrible it must be, to feel so helpless.

"Not on the nightstand, but I'll find them in a minute or two, I'm sure." She checked the bed first, to be sure they hadn't become tangled with the covers, and then began working her way around the room. The glasses finally turned up on the mantel over the disused fireplace, tucked behind a framed picture of Matthew Dixon and his wife on their wedding day.

"Here they are. They were on the mantel."

He slid them on and peered at her, blue eyes sharp. "He hid them, that's what he did. Doesn't like me getting around on my own."

"I'm sure Andy wouldn't do that." She found a pair of black lace-up shoes in the closet and helped him put on socks and shoes.

He stood, grasping her shoulder for a moment. "You're a good girl. I'm going downstairs now."

She slipped around to his side, ready to grab him if he seemed tottery, but he went down the stairs as spryly as a younger man.

"Come on into the kitchen. I need some coffee. You can tell me what you want." He headed briskly to the kitchen, confident now, a complete change from the helpless soul he'd been a few minutes before.

He poured two mugs of coffee from the modern coffeemaker that looked out of place on the worn wooden counter and shoved one toward her. She took a sip of coffee strong enough to make her hair stand on end. Dixon downed his with every indication of enjoyment.

"Now then." The coffee seemed to complete his transformation. He stood erect, looking at her questioningly. "What was it you wanted?"

"It's about the Ortiz family—from the migrant worker camp. Their daughter has been helping us at the clinic, and we'd like to see her have a chance to attend school here for a while. If you could hire her father to stay through the apple harvest—"

But he was already shaking his head. "It's none of my concern. That's taken care of by the crew chief."

"You're the employer, Mr. Dixon. Surely, if you said you wanted them to stay, the crew chief would go along with you." She was losing him already, the rapport she'd thought she'd built slipping away.

His face tightened. "Why are you bothering me with this? The farm workers aren't any of your concern."

"They have to be somebody's concern." She felt her temper slipping and tried to grasp control.

"You and your do-gooders." His face reddened. "I should have known better than to agree to that clinic."

"They need the clinic. They need better housing, too. You should be ashamed of the conditions they're living in." So much for controlling her temper. She'd end up regretting this, but somebody had to confront him about his treatment of the workers.

He slammed his cup down on the table so hard it was a wonder it didn't smash to pieces. "You're out of line, young woman. My workers have everything they need. My son sees to that."

"That's not what Andy—"

He didn't let her finish. "I'll thank you to get out of my house and mind your own business."

"Taking care of other people is everyone's business."

"Out!" His face was so red that she was afraid to pursue it any further.

She turned toward the door. "Please. Just think about it." She didn't dare say more. She went quickly down the hall and out of the house.

It wasn't until she was driving down the lane that she realized she was shaking, her hands trembling so that she had to grip the wheel to steer.

She'd failed. She never should have thought she could deal with Dixon herself. She'd just made the whole thing worse.

And if Dixon complained to Jake, or worse, to the hospital board, she might have created more trouble than any of them could handle.

Chapter Twelve

Terry rubbed the polishing rag along the chrome trim of the rig. The firehouse was quiet, with most on-duty personnel upstairs having lunch. The quiet suited her. She and Jeff had decided the rig needed a thorough cleaning, and the routine chore combined with the quiet soothed her.

Jeff was inside the rig, taking inventory of their supplies. His tuneless whistle was part of the background to her thoughts. Unfortunately, letting her mind stray from how many inches of chrome she had to polish was a good recipe for disturbing her mood.

She was certainly better off here than trying to intercede on Manuela's behalf. She'd messed that up thoroughly when she'd tried to talk to Dixon about her.

Her polishing cloth slowed its circular movements. She'd been waiting for the shoe to drop for over twenty-four hours—waiting for an irate call from Jake or a stern one from the hospital board. So far, nothing had happened. Apparently Mr. Dixon hadn't complained about her. Yet.

Ripping off a paper towel, she wiped down the headlight, running the towel into the seam. Odd, what Dixon had said about letting Andy handle everything to do with the migrant worker housing. That hadn't been the impression Andy gave.

Maybe the truth lay somewhere in between. Perhaps the elder Dixon gave Andy the work, but without the authority to make any changes. Fathers and sons seemed to have far more complicated relationships than mothers and daughters, from what she could see.

She might never really know the answer. Andy didn't have any reason to confide in her, even if he did claim friendship from kindergarten.

And as far as confiding was concerned, she had some of that to do. She ought to have told Brendan what happened with Dixon. Maybe he could come up with some other way to help the Ortiz family.

And she ought to tell Jake, as well. Her throat tightened at the thought of forcing those words out. He would not be happy with her. He'd warned her to tread cautiously with Dixon, and she'd plunged in as if everything depended on her.

If Dixon decided to complain, she'd put the work of the clinic in jeopardy. And even if he didn't, her actions might mean that he wouldn't agree to allow the clinic access to his workers next year.

Jake felt that any complaint about the clinic could reflect on him. She found it hard to believe that the board would refuse him a permanent contract based on her mistakes, but what mattered was what Jake believed. She had to confess to him, and the sooner, the better.

"Are you Ms. Flanagan?"

She straightened so sharply she nearly cracked her head on the rearview mirror. She had been so deep in thought that she hadn't heard the woman approach, although those high heels must have made noise on the concrete floor.

Fashionable, expensive heels, matching an equally expensive leather bag. A lightweight gray suit that echoed perfectly coiffed gray hair. This was not the sort of person one expected to find in the firehouse.

"I'm Terry Flanagan. May I help you?"

The woman let her gaze drift over Terry from head to foot, and Terry found herself squaring her shoulders. Okay, maybe she didn't look like a fashion plate in her paramedic uniform, with a cleaning rag in her hand. She didn't intend to.

"I'm Lila Landsdowne. Is there someplace we can speak? In private." She frowned at Jeff, whose startled face had appeared in the window above her.

Lila Landsdowne. Jake's mother—she had to be. Terry's stomach tied itself into knots. This couldn't be good. What did Jake's mother want with her?

"Well—" She looked around, finding nothing suitable for a private talk in the engine room. Besides, she wasn't sure she wanted a private talk with Jake's mother. Did he know she was here?

Jeff slid out of the rig. "I'll go up and have lunch, Ter. I'll make sure nobody comes down to bother you." He gave Mrs. Landsdowne an awkward nod and hurried toward the stairs.

The woman let her gaze follow him until he was out of sight. Then she turned back to Terry, one silvery eyebrow lifted.

She was not going to let the woman intimidate her.

This was her place. She managed a smile. "We'll be private enough here. I'm afraid there's no place to sit, unless you'd like to get into the rig."

A pained expression crossed Mrs. Landsdowne's face. "No. This will do. I understand you're a friend of my son's."

"Did Jake tell you that?" This visit seemed odd, to say the least.

"No." Her lips tightened, lines showing beneath perfect makeup. "I haven't spoken to Jacob in some time."

"Then how—"

"Really, Ms. Flanagan, we're wasting time. I make it my business to know what my son is doing. I know about your relationship." She looked as if the words left a bad taste in her mouth.

"Jake and I are friends," Terry said carefully. "That's all."

"If that's true, I'm sure you'll see the wisdom of doing what I ask."

"What would that be?"

"I want you to encourage him to come back to Boston, where he belongs, and take up the position his father has arranged for him."

Terry could only stare at her for a moment. Mrs. Landsdowne looked at her with, apparently, every expectation that Terry would accede to anything she wanted.

"I'm sorry. I can't do that."

"Can't?" She looked as if no one had ever said the word to her before.

"It's Jake's decision, not mine. It's none of my business." She had no doubt that Jake would agree with that sentiment.

"Don't play games with me." Her voice sharpened. "I've been told you have influence over Jacob. I'm asking you to use it."

Her patience was fraying. "Your source is wrong. And if I did have influence over him, I wouldn't use it."

The woman blinked. Her lips pressed together for an instant, and then she produced something that might be a smile. "I suppose I'm approaching this all wrong. I didn't mean to offend you."

Oh yes, you did, she thought, and was instantly ashamed. She owed Mrs. Landsdowne courtesy, if nothing else. "I'm not offended. There's just nothing I can do."

"I suppose you know that Jacob's father tried to talk to him about this." She shook her head. "Really, I should have known those two couldn't talk without putting each other's back up."

"I wouldn't know about that."

"No, of course you don't know Jacob's family, his background." She gave an indulgent smile. "Jacob and his father are too alike. Both of them so gifted, so intense. Naturally they disagree, but really, they belong together."

She was out of her depth, and she knew it. She could hardly argue that she knew Jake better than his family. She could only say what she believed to be true. "Jake doesn't seem to think so."

"He's hurt, poor boy. He's had a difficult time, you must know that." She reached out to grasp Terry's hand. "Now he has a chance to put all that behind him and take his rightful place—the only place where he can use his talents to the fullest."

"I don't—"

"Now, don't say no." She pressed her hand persua-

sively. "You must understand, Ms. Flanagan. My
husband is not a well man. He needs Jacob to return, but
he's too proud to tell him that. You'll tell him, won't
you? You don't have to try and persuade him of
anything. Just tell him what I said."

She had a sense of being swept away on a riptide.
"Why don't you tell him yourself?"

"It'll be better coming from you." She patted her
hand and turned away. "You're his friend. I know you
don't want Jake to spend his life regretting that he didn't
respond when his father needed him. I know you'll do
the right thing."

She turned and walked away before Terry could
come up with a single thing to say.

Because there wasn't anything to say. She watched
the outside door close behind Jacob's mother. If Jake's
father was seriously ill—well, she couldn't take the
responsibility of keeping that from him. But somehow
she doubted that their friendship was going to survive
everything she had to tell him.

Jake tossed the remains of his frozen dinner into the
trash and wandered into the living room. In his first days
in Suffolk, he'd welcomed the privacy and isolation of
his evenings off. The condo was his sanctuary. Now he
felt oddly restless, and he thought he knew the cause.

Terry. He glanced toward the telephone. He hadn't
seen her in two days, and her absence made a bigger
hole in his life than he'd have imagined possible.

She'd tried so hard to help him over that business
with his father. He felt his jaw tighten at the thought of
his father's visit, and he had to deliberately relax it.

Terry hadn't understood their relationship. Well, how could she, growing up with the family she had? She probably didn't know how lucky she was.

Still, he appreciated the fact that she'd tried, the fact that she'd cared. Terry, with that warm, open heart of hers, was proving to be a force to be reckoned with in his life.

In spite of his determination to concentrate on nothing but his job, she'd drawn him in—into the clinic, into her caring about Manuela's future, even into her family. Knowing her had even made him more aware of his relationship with God. Who would guess that one little red-haired whirlwind could have such an effect?

He was actually reaching for the telephone when the doorbell chimed. Somehow, even before he swung the door open, he knew who he'd see.

Terry had changed from her uniform into a denim skirt and sunny yellow top, with a sweater slung over her shoulders against the evening cool, a reminder that fall was on its way.

"How did you manage that?" He gestured her in and closed the door. "I was just thinking of you, and here you are."

"I hope you don't mind." Her fingers twisted the sleeve end of her sweater. "I wanted to talk to you, and I thought it would be better away from the hospital."

"Sounds serious." But he didn't feel serious, not when just looking at her brought a smile to his lips.

She frowned, as if considering. "I'm not sure how serious it is. I have a couple of things to tell you, and I don't think you're going to like either of them."

She looked like a guilty kid, standing in front of the principal's desk. He'd never minded inspiring a little fear in his subordinates, but somehow he didn't want Terry looking at him that way.

"Let's sit down and have it out, whatever it is." He led her to the sofa and sat down next to her. "Come on. Spill it."

She folded her hands in her lap, took a deep breath and met his gaze. "Your mother came to see me today at the firehouse."

He couldn't do anything but stare at her. "My mother. Are you sure?" He knew how ridiculous that was as soon as he said the words.

But at least it made her smile a little. "Late fifties, silver hair, better dressed than anyone who's ever come into the firehouse, I'd guess. You have her eyes, don't you?"

"I suppose so." The collision of what he'd considered two separate worlds boggled the mind. Still, since his father had failed, it was reasonable to expect his mother to try. That was how they always worked. But… "Why did she come to see you? How does she even know about you?"

Terry shrugged, clearly uncomfortable. "I don't know. I asked her how she knew we were friends, and she just said that naturally she kept tabs on her son."

"I don't know what's natural about it. They cut me out of their lives pretty thoroughly when I disappointed them." Anger smoldered along his veins. Who in Suffolk could be his mother's source of information? Dr. Getz?

"I tried to get out of talking to her. Really I did. She just wouldn't take no for an answer."

Her distress touched him, and he put his hand over hers. "It's not your fault. I know what my mother is like.

If she wanted to say something, you wouldn't be able to stop her." He managed a smile. "You're too well-brought-up to be outright rude, and even that wouldn't stop her."

"I still didn't like it. Feeling as if we were talking about you behind your back."

"What did she want?" He thought he already knew.

"She wanted me to persuade you to accept your father's offer."

"How did she think you could do that?"

Terry shook her head, obviously distressed. "I don't know. I told her no, of course."

"But you're here."

"I couldn't keep it from you. She said that you and your father always disagree, but it's just because you're so alike."

"Alike? I used to think so. Now I know that's the exact opposite of what I want to be." Once the words were out, he looked at them in astonishment. He'd never thought of his feelings toward his father in just that way.

Terry's face was somber. "She said—well, she implied—that your father is seriously ill. That he really needs you to come home, but was too proud to tell you."

"Terry—" How did he explain this to her? People like his parents were out of her realm. "They've been doing this my whole life. They each have their own way of getting me to do what they want. This is just another example of that."

"How can you be sure?" She clasped his hand in both of hers. "What if he really is sick? You can't just ignore it, even if you decide you can't do what he wants."

Her passion touched him. "Why does it matter so much to you?"

"Because I don't want you to do something you'll regret later."

"I know." He brushed her cheek with his fingertips, seeing the flood of warm color where they touched. "But why does it matter to you?"

It probably wasn't fair to put her on the spot that way—to ask for a declaration of caring from her before he was ready to do the same.

She met his gaze steadily. "Because I care about you. I want what's best for you."

"Terry—" His voice choked a little. "I don't deserve that kind of caring."

A smile trembled on her lips. "I can't help it."

He pressed his palm against her cheek, letting the silk of her hair flow across his fingers. She was so warm, so giving, and he was drawn to her as a freezing man seeks the fire.

He lowered his lips toward hers, and even while telling himself that he shouldn't, he kissed her. Her lips were soft and sweet against his. She leaned into his kiss with such trust and tenderness that his doubts slid away as if they'd never been.

She pulled back, so suddenly that his hand still touched her cheek. She shook her head, eyes troubled, soft curls moving against his hand. "I can't."

Easy—take it easy. "Why? We're both free, aren't we?"

"It's not that." She drew away from him, running a hand through her tousled hair. "It's just—you're not going to feel like kissing me when you've heard the rest of it."

Somehow he doubted that anything could take away his longing to hold her. "Maybe you'd better tell me, whatever it is. Did you agree to kidnap me and ship me back to my mother?"

She didn't smile in response. "I went to see Matthew Dixon."

"Dixon—I thought we were going to let Andy handle that."

"Andy hasn't done anything. I'm not sure he ever would." Her eyes brimmed with sudden tears. "I'm sorry. Dad always says I rush in where angels fear to tread. I thought I could make him see how important it is to Manuela that her parents stay."

"It doesn't sound as if you succeeded." There was little point in getting angry with Terry. She'd only done what was in her nature to do. He couldn't accept the fullness of her loving heart for himself and deny it to others.

"At first he seemed glad I was there." She frowned. "It was rather odd, as a matter of fact. He was alone upstairs, and he couldn't find his glasses. Apparently he can't see well enough even to get around the house without them."

"And you helped him." Of course.

She nodded. "He acted as if Andy had hidden his glasses on purpose. But then he turned around and insisted Andy was in charge of the migrant farm workers, and he refused to interfere."

"And he was angry at your interference." Angry enough to complain to the board?

"That was yesterday afternoon. Surely if he was going to make a complaint, he'd have done it by now." Terry obviously knew what his immediate thought would be.

"Let's hope so." He squeezed her hand. "Don't look so upset. If necessary, I'll talk to Dr. Getz about it. He has influence with the board and with Dixon."

"You're not angry?"

"No." Surprisingly, he wasn't. He stood, pulling her up with him. "But I think maybe you'd better go. Being alone with you here isn't the greatest thing for my self-control."

Her dimples showed. "Or mine." She started toward the door, then turned back just as she reached it. "I'm sorry if I've made things more difficult for you."

"It's okay."

She studied his face, as if to be sure he was telling the truth. "You will call your mother, won't you? Just talk to her."

If he didn't, Terry would take the burden of that on herself. "I'll call. I promise." But he wouldn't promise to believe everything he heard.

"Good night."

He wouldn't cross the room to her, because if he did, he'd end up kissing her again. "Good night, Terry. Don't worry so much. Everything is going to work out."

But when the door had closed behind her, his smile slid away. *Everything is going to work out.* He just wished he could believe that.

Terry smiled at the six-year-old who'd come to the clinic for a colorful bandage on a scraped knee. "There you go, buddy. Next time look before you run."

The little boy flashed a smile when Manuela translated the words. *"Muchas gracias,"* he said, and trotted happily toward the door.

Manuela shook her head disapprovingly, the single braid of her hair bouncing against her shoulders. She'd started wearing her hair that way after commenting on the braid Terry usually wore when working.

"He did not need to bother you with that. He just wants to show off to his friends that he was treated at the clinic."

"That's fine." Terry soaped her hands thoroughly. "That's what we want, you see. To have all the children feel comfortable about coming to us."

"I see. I did not think of that. But most of us will leave in a few days. There probably won't be a clinic at the next camp." She didn't ask the obvious question, but it was there in her dark eyes.

Terry dried her hands slowly, buying time. She hated to have to tell Manuela the truth, but the girl had a right to know. It was her future, after all.

"I'm sorry, Manuela." She touched her shoulder lightly. "I talked to Mr. Dixon myself, but I didn't have any success in getting him to agree to keep your father on. I wish I had better news for you."

The girl's eyes went bright with tears, but she didn't let them spill over. "It's all right." She lifted her head, as if trying to say that it didn't matter. "I knew it was too much to hope."

Terry's heart twisted. It shouldn't be too much to hope that a smart girl would have a chance at an education. Manuela was such a hard worker. She deserved better than bouncing from camp to camp for the next few months, falling further and further behind in her schoolwork.

"I know most of the crew will be going to North Carolina next, and then working their way south." There was no way of knowing what Manuela would think of Mom's idea without asking her. That was the first step, in any event. "If it were possible for you to stay here without your family to attend school until they go back to Mexico, would you want to do it?"

Hope flared in Manuela's face, but she seemed to force herself to tamp it down. "How could that be? Would the government let me stay with someone else? Who would I stay with?"

"I don't know about the legal situation. My cousin Brendan is working on finding that out. But if it is allowed, my parents would invite you to stay with us and go to school, if you wanted to."

"I would want, yes. But my mother—I don't know how she would get along without me to help her. And my father depends on me to speak English for him."

She was obviously torn, and Terry could only honor her for thinking of her family's needs first, instead of her own desires. For that matter, she felt torn, too, not knowing whether what she was suggesting for Manuela was the right thing.

Please, Father, guide both of us to make the right choices.

"You'd have to decide that. Talk to them about it, too. But until we know if it's legally possible, maybe you should wait."

Manuela nodded. Maybe she was thinking that this, too, was an impossible dream.

"Whether this works out or not, I want you to know that you have friends here who want to help you. Will you believe that?"

Tears glistened in her eyes again. "I will. Thank you."

Before she could say more, the clinic door opened. The way her nerve endings jumped to attention told her it was Jake almost before she looked. He stopped at the

registration desk, greeting the volunteers, before sauntering casually in her direction.

No, not so casually. She could detect tension in the
way he moved, in the fine lines around his mouth. She
waited until he'd spoken briefly to Manuela, until the
girl moved away to help someone else.

"Is something wrong?"

Please, don't let this be a problem that I caused.
Maybe that's selfish, but I don't want to be a source of
trouble for Jake. I want to help him.

"Not wrong, exactly."

He took the schedule of volunteers from its hook on
the wall and seemed to be studying it, but she could see
that his mind was preoccupied. Obviously he didn't
want to appear to be having a private conversation with
her during clinic hours. She began tidying up the first
aid supplies.

"But not right, either?" she asked quietly.

He frowned down at the clipboard in his hand. "I
talked with my mother. My father has been having some
heart symptoms. Nothing as serious as she implied to
you, but certainly he should slow down. He keeps a
surgery schedule that would tire a man half his age."

It was a struggle to keep her voice even, ensuring that
the anxiety she felt didn't show in her voice. "I suppose
she asked you to come back to Boston."

He nodded. "That was the crux of it. The startling
thing was that my father came on the phone and actually
apologized for his manner the last time we talked. My
father never apologizes."

"Maybe discovering that he's not made of steel had
a humbling effect on him." She had to think of what was

best for Jake, not of her longing to have him stay. "I guess he realizes that he needs you."

Jake's lips tightened. "He doesn't need me. Any bright young neurosurgeon would be delighted to come into his practice. He wants me because he's always wanted to build a dynasty."

Her heart hurt for him. He was still wounded over his family's rejection of him when he needed them most. No wonder he found it hard to consider going back now.

"You can't be sure of his motives. I know your relationship has been painful, but maybe he really does regret his actions."

Don't go, Jake. That was what she really wanted to say. Don't go. Stay here, with me.

"I don't know." Jake's frown deepened, setting harsh lines in his face. "I'm trying to be fair to them, but it's not easy. This whole Christian forgiveness thing is a tough one."

"I know." Maybe you have to forgive yourself, first. She wanted to say it, but she feared his reaction. "What did you tell them?"

"I said I'd think about it." He shot her a look that was baffled, almost angry. "How am I supposed to know what to do? I turned my life and my career over to God, but He doesn't seem to be providing any answers."

"He will." She believed that with all her heart. "Pray and wait. He'll make it clear, in His time."

And if Jake decided that he was going back to Boston? She wouldn't attempt to prevent him. She'd find some way to say goodbye with a smile, even though her heart would be breaking.

Chapter Thirteen

The conversation with his parents still lurked uneasily in the back of Jake's mind the next day. Surprisingly, he no longer felt the anger with them that he'd battled for months. That was a good thing, even though he had no intention of taking up his father's offer.

Or did he? The delicate dance of the operating room still had its appeal, but he wasn't sure whether he'd wanted it because it was his special gift or because it had been drummed into him from the time he could talk.

That visit of his mother's to Terry still seemed odd to him. His mother had skillfully evaded his questions on the subject, leaving him no wiser than before he'd talked to her. There was no link between the Beacon Hill house and Suffolk, or at least that's what he'd thought when he'd come here.

Ahead of him in the hospital corridor, he spotted Sam Getz's portly figure turning into the doctors' lounge. Links, connections—well, there was one, if you looked at it that way. Dr. Getz had known his father, years ago.

Acting on impulse, he turned toward the lounge. Maybe Dr. Getz would say what his mother had not. Getz could, he supposed, have told his parents about Terry, although he couldn't imagine a reason why he would. Surely, as far as Getz was concerned, his only relationship with Terry was that of supervisor at the clinic.

And what is your relationship with Terry? The voice in the back of his mind pricked him. The truth was that he didn't know the answer to that question. But whatever he felt for her, it was complicating the decisions he made about his future.

Without Terry's prodding, he might never have called his mother. And she'd been right—if he hadn't made that effort, he'd have regretted it someday. Now, no matter what decision he ultimately made, he'd know he'd at least tried to mend the breach between them.

He reached the lounge door and paused, hand on the knob. His father would probably say he was letting his emotions cloud his judgment again. Maybe so, but he wanted to know what had led his mother to Terry Flanagan.

The door opened with a faint swish, and Dr. Getz glanced toward him from the counter where he stood, stirring his coffee. His round face broke into a smile.

"Jake, I hoped I'd run into you today. There's something I want to ask you."

"Of course, Dr. Getz." He crossed the room, wondering if he could possibly stomach yet another cup of coffee today. Maybe not. At least Getz didn't look as if he were the bearer of bad news. "What is it?"

Getz leaned against the counter, mug held between his hands. "I was wondering about your father. I understand he's been having some health problems."

Now how had he heard that? "Nothing serious, sir, but thank you for asking. How did you happen to hear about it?"

The older man shrugged. "The medical grapevine is alive and well. And more active than ever, thanks to the Internet. I happened to be e-mailing back and forth with the person who's trying to set up a med school class reunion. She mentioned it. Seems she'd heard that you were going into practice with him, since he's not well."

And that was probably what the chief of staff really wanted to know. Are you going to leave us?

"My father did make that suggestion," he said carefully. He couldn't lie to the man, but he didn't want to burn any bridges in Suffolk. "I told him that I'm happy here. I don't have any plans to change my career path at the moment."

"Well, good." Getz beamed. "I don't want to lose you, either. It can be hard to find someone who has the gifts we need and settles so easily into small town life."

"Suffolk's a good place." Just ask him. He's not going to take offense. "Speaking of the grapevine, I wondered if you happened to say anything to my father about Terry Flanagan."

Getz's gaze slid away from his, and he actually looked embarrassed. "I hope I didn't speak out of turn. Truth to tell, I find your father a bit hard to talk to, and I was trying to make conversation. Was that a problem?"

"Not at all. I just didn't want my parents to get the wrong idea about our relationship."

"I don't think I implied anything but friendship. I'm pleased that you've made friends with the Flanagan family. They're good people."

"Yes, they are." So Getz had probably mentioned Terry, his father had repeated it to his mother, and she'd added two and two and come up with sixteen, afraid he was getting involved with someone she'd consider inappropriate.

"You know…" Getz began and then stopped. He shook his head. "I've been debating all day about whether to mention something to you. But I guess maybe you should know."

He tensed. Had Dixon been stirring up trouble?

"Something about the clinic?"

"No, no, nothing to do with that. Well, the fact is, there are rumors circulating around the hospital. Rumors about why you left Philadelphia."

For a moment he was speechless. That was the last thing he'd expected to hear. "I—what are they saying about me?"

Getz flushed. "Talking about your relationship with the young woman who died. Now, you were perfectly honest with me when we hired you, and I know you weren't to blame. But you know what hospital grapevines are like."

He knew only too well. His memories of just how bad it had been in Philadelphia were still strong in his mind. He'd hated the feeling that everyone was talking about him, feeling as if he were enmeshed in a sticky spiderweb of innuendo and half-truth, impossible to fight.

"I thought I'd be free of that here."

Getz put a fatherly hand on his shoulder. "I understand, but you can't let it get you down. I've tried to scotch any rumors I've heard, but that just means they'll be careful not to talk in front of me. The best thing you can do is ignore it."

That was good advice, but probably impossible to take. Still, what could he do? He couldn't go around telling his side of the story to half the hospital, the way he'd told it to Terry.

Terry. Terry was the only person in Suffolk who knew about his past.

Terry pushed Michael on the swing at the park, smiling when his face broke into a wide grin. "Okay, you need to pump now if you want to go higher. Do it the way Shawna does." She nodded toward Michael's big sister, who'd already pumped high enough to take Terry's breath away.

"It's more fun when you push me," Michael complained, but he struggled manfully to match his sister's height.

Terry took a few steps back, watching them. She'd been surprised when Mary Kate called and asked her to pick the kids up from school and keep them busy for an hour or so. Mary Kate didn't often ask for help.

Not only had she asked, she'd actually admitted, to her kid sister, of all people, that she was feeling low today and didn't want Mom to know.

Perhaps her talk with Mary Kate hadn't been so futile after all. If her big sis could admit she needed help once in a while, maybe they could move to a more equal relationship.

"Hey, Aunt Terry, look who's coming!"

If it was Mary Kate, coming to check up on her— But it wasn't. Instead, she saw Jake coming across the grass toward them. Her heart gave that little jolt it always did when she saw him, but today it was muted by apprehension. Was he planning to tell her that he'd decided to accept his father's offer?

"Hi, Shawna. Michael. Are you trying to see how high you can go?"

He actually remembered their names, even though he'd only met them once, as far as she knew. She sensed something distracted behind the smile he turned on the kids.

"They're trying to give their aunt a heart attack, that's what they're doing," she said. She grabbed Michael's swing. "Okay, you two. Go join the crowd on the sliding board for a while."

Michael frowned, but when Shawna hopped nimbly off her swing and darted toward the sliding board, red curls bouncing, he followed her. She watched them run, reminded again of their loss. Michael had been especially close to his father, and his usual sunny disposition had undergone a change since Kenny's death.

"They're cute kids." Jake seemed to be watching them, too. "How is your sister doing?"

"Not bad. She was feeling a bit down today, so she asked me to pick up the kids. She never wants them to see her cry."

"It must be tough."

He sounded sympathetic, but she sensed that his mind was elsewhere.

They might as well get this over with, whatever it was. She swung to face him. The place where they stood, under the shade of an oak tree behind the swings, was as private a spot as any, despite the running children and the mothers with strollers over near the sandbox.

"What is it, Jake? I can see that something's wrong."

He didn't bother to deny it. "I had a little chat with Dr. Getz this afternoon."

Apprehension made her fingers clench. "Was it Dixon? Did he complain about me?"

"No. It wasn't that."

He stopped, frowning, and she had the sense that he'd moved away from her. His guard was up in a way she hadn't seen in weeks. The rapport she'd felt recently, even when they were arguing about something, had vanished. She was suddenly chilled, despite the warmth of the day.

"What is it, then? Did Getz call you in about something else?" Just tell me, please.

"He didn't call me in. I saw him going in the lounge, and I caught up with him. I wanted to know if he was the one who told my parents about you."

It took a moment to adjust her thoughts, so much had happened since that odd interview with Jake's mother at the firehouse.

"What difference does it make how they found out about me? I told your mother that I wouldn't attempt to influence you."

His mouth set. "I don't like the idea that someone's spying on me. Talking about you to them."

Why, Jake? Are you ashamed of our relationship? She didn't need him to tell her that she wasn't the kind of woman they wanted for their only son.

"I wasn't bothered by it." That wasn't quite true, but she didn't know what else to say. She could hardly tell him that she didn't appreciate his mother looking down on her.

"I was. I don't like the idea of my mother going to my friends behind my back."

"What did Dr. Getz say?"

"He admitted that he probably mentioned you and your family to my father when he was here. I'm sure my mother filled in the rest of the blanks without any trouble."

She still didn't understand why it bothered him so much. She tried to imagine her mother going to one of her friends in an attempt to manipulate her, but the image just made her smile.

"That wasn't the worst of it." Jake's voice hardened. "Dr. Getz told me something else. He said that rumors are making the rounds of the hospital."

He made it sound so dire.

"If people are talking about our friendship—" she began.

"Not that." His tone dismissed their friendship as if it were of no importance. "Rumors about Meredith's death. Rumors blaming me for it."

Her breath caught. It was so unexpected that she couldn't speak for a moment. "Jake, I'm so sorry." Tears filled her eyes, and she blinked them back. "I don't understand. How could that have happened? I thought no one here knew about that except Dr. Getz, and he certainly wouldn't have said anything."

"No. He wouldn't."

"But then how—"

"One other person knew." His face was very still. "You knew, Terry."

It was as if he'd struck her. "You can't believe that I'd do that."

"I don't want to believe it."

"Don't you?" Anger came to her rescue, holding the pain at bay for the moment, at least. "You look as if you do."

"I don't." To do him credit, making the accusation did seem to cause him pain—pain that he held behind that stony mask he wore. "But I can't argue with the facts. You were the only one who knew. Now everyone knows. What am I supposed to believe?"

The anger seeped away too quickly, leaving only the hurt. "I don't know, Jake. I think you might trust me as a friend, if nothing else." Her mind winced away from the kisses they'd shared. "But I guess I'd be wrong, wouldn't I?"

She could only turn away, trying to keep him from seeing how much he'd hurt her. He stood for another moment, but he didn't speak. And then he walked quickly away.

"Here you go." Terry forced a smile when Mary Kate opened the door. "Two kids, safe and sound."

Mary Kate hugged them, and only the very observant could detect the faint redness around her eyes. The dusting of flour on her jeans and the scent of baking said she must have worked through her sorrow. "Did you have fun with Aunt Terry?"

"I went down the big slide," Shawna announced. "And we saw Dr. Jake, too. He came to talk to Aunt Terry."

Mary Kate sent a questioning glance her way, seeming to register all the things Terry had no intention of saying to her. "Okay, you guys." She gave the children a little shove toward the kitchen. "Milk and oatmeal cookies are on the table."

"Oatmeal cookies!" They shouted it in chorus and raced for the kitchen, immediately beginning an argument over whose cookies were bigger.

"Good luck." Terry turned. The only thing she wanted right now was to be alone and lick her wounds.

Her sister grabbed her arm. "Not so fast. What's wrong?"

"Nothing." She tried to pull free.

Mary Kate just tightened her grasp. "Don't kid me, Ter. I've had too much practice trying to hide my feelings not to know when you're doing it. Besides, you helped me. Give me a chance to return the favor."

She let Mary Kate pull her inside. "There's nothing you can do." She grimaced. "Nothing I can do, either."

"Jake, I guess, from what the kids said."

She nodded, blinking away the tears that wanted to fill her eyes. "You know, I really thought we were getting someplace. I thought—" She stopped, shrugged. "Well, it doesn't matter, because I was wrong."

Mary Kate put a comforting arm around her shoulder. "Are you sure? Judging by the way I've seen him look at you, he has feelings for you."

"Feelings, maybe. But not enough to trust me." Bitterness left an acrid taste in her mouth. "He found out rumors are circulating around the hospital about him. About something that happened in Philadelphia that he thinks only I know. So of course he jumped to the conclusion that I gossiped about him."

"Well, that's just plain stupid. Anyone who knows you knows you can be trusted."

Mary Kate's anger was heartening.

"I guess he doesn't know me, then." She shook her

head. "Thanks for listening, M.K., but there's nothing anybody can do about it. I just thought—" The tears welled again, silencing her.

"You love him."

She nodded. "Dumb, huh?"

"He's the one who's dumb." Mary Kate's tone grew brisk, so that she almost sounded like Mom. "But don't you tell me you can't do anything. You've never admitted in your life that there was a problem you can't do anything about."

"This is different."

Her sister gave her a little shake. "Come on, you know better than that. You wouldn't put up with anyone else being unjustly accused. Why would you take it for yourself?"

She blinked at Mary Kate's vehemence. "You know what? You're right." She gave her sister a quick kiss on the cheek. "I'm going to the hospital right now, and I'm not leaving until I know who started this stupid rumor."

"Good for you." Mary Kate smiled. "Now that's our Terry talking."

Propelled by a wave of righteous indignation, she started for the car. She'd find out whose fault this was, and she'd give that person a piece of her mind.

It was nearly two hours later when she trudged down the hallway toward the E.R. She'd been over half the hospital, it seemed, questioning people, tracing the garbled story from one person to another, trying to do damage control as she went.

But it was no good. Once started, a rumor was like a stubborn weed that sent up new sprouts each time you cut one down. She couldn't reveal the things Jake had confided in her, and there was just enough of a seed of truth to make it impossible to fight without revealing everything.

She'd done what she set out to do. She'd tracked the story down to its source, but knowing wasn't giving her any pleasure.

Harriet was on duty in the E.R. She stood in the hallway, conferring with a nurse, but when she saw Terry she handed over the chart she held and started toward her.

"Hi. I didn't expect to see you back here today. I thought you were off duty."

"I am. How about a cup of coffee?" She tried to manage a smile, but it was no good. She couldn't, not knowing what she did.

Harriet blinked at her tone, and then she led the way into the break room—empty, thank goodness. The door swung shut behind them.

"What's wrong?" Harriet frowned at her. "I can see there's something. Is it the clinic?"

"No." Her throat went tight. What if she were wrong—but she wasn't. "Why did you do it, Harriet? Why did you tell people about Jake and what happened in Philadelphia?"

For a moment Harriet just stared at her, and she knew their friendship was on the line. If Harriet denied it…

Finally Harriet shook her head, her gaze sliding away. Her shoulders slumped under the white lab coat. "How did you find out it was me?"

It took an effort to swallow. "I just kept asking people. Every trail led back to you. Why? And how did you even know about it?"

She shrugged, still not looking at Terry. "Our medical world isn't that big, is it? I knew someone who'd been an intern at the hospital when Landsdowne was there. I gave him a call. He was only too happy to pass along what everyone said about why Landsdowne left."

"Gossip." She wished she had enough energy to be angry with Harriet. "You know as well as anyone that the story probably got added to and embellished by everyone who repeated it. Why would you do such a thing?"

"Why would you defend him?" Harriet's anger flared. "I thought you disliked having him here. That's certainly what you said when he came."

She had to be careful. She couldn't violate Jake's privacy, even to clear him. "We had our problems, yes. But that doesn't mean I'd set out to sabotage him. Why, Harriet? That's what I don't get. Why did you go to all that trouble to hurt him?"

Harriet's hands tightened into fists. "Why? Because I should have gotten that job, not some outsider brought in just because Getz went to med school with his father. It's not fair. The old boys' network wins every time."

This, at least, she could clear up. "You're wrong, Harriet. That's not why Getz wanted him. I heard him myself. He chose Jake because he admired his work in Somalia. Maybe that's not the reason he should have hired someone, but it didn't have anything to do with his father's influence." Despair swept over her. She was losing her friend. "If someone had told me you'd do this, I wouldn't have believed it. Not of you."

For a moment longer Harriet stared at her, angry. Then, slowly, her expression changed. She put her hand up to her forehead, shielding her eyes. The hand shook a little.

"When you put it that way, I guess I don't believe it of myself." Her hand dropped, and she faced Terry, tears sparkling in her eyes. "You're right. I've been telling myself I was justified, but—" Her mouth twisted. "I'm sorry. What can I do to make it right?"

That was a question that didn't seem to have much of an answer. "I suppose you can try to tell people that the story was just gossip, but I don't suppose it will do much good."

She was suddenly tired, too tired to go on struggling with this. No matter what Harriet did now, even if she went to Jake and confessed—it didn't really matter. The bottom line was that he hadn't trusted her, and the relationship she'd thought they had was nothing but a sham.

Chapter Fourteen

Jake managed a smile for the small girl he'd just immunized and nodded to Manuela. "Make sure the mother understands that the vitamins are not candy. She's to give each child one each day, and keep the bottles where they can't get them."

Thanks to the generosity of Brendan's church, when the migrant families left tomorrow, each child would have a two-month supply of vitamins, in addition to having their immunizations up to date. And thanks to Manuela, he didn't have to worry about making a mistake with the instructions.

So far, he'd managed to spend over an hour at the clinic without crossing paths with Terry. She had her own station across the room, helping to give well-baby checkups, and she was probably just as happy to avoid him.

He'd spend the past two days at the hospital trying to ignore the whispered conversations that cut off abruptly when he walked by. It wasn't easy.

He could just imagine what his father would do in this situation, not that that would ever happen. His father would blithely ignore the talk, confident as always in his own judgment, not swayed by what anyone else thought or said.

As for him—well, once again he'd let his emotions get in the way of his good judgment. He'd let his feelings for Terry override his self-control, and look where that had gotten him.

Almost without willing it, he glanced toward her. She was smiling at a baby who reached, entranced, for a red curl that had come loose from her braid. Just as quickly, he looked away, his heart twisting. Terry probably hadn't spilled his secret deliberately, but the result had been the same.

The whispers followed him, and sooner or later they'd reach the hospital board. Dr. Getz had interviewed him—Dr. Getz had heard the whole story and hired him anyway. But if the board started demanding answers—well, maybe he should accept his father's offer before this whole thing exploded in his face.

Manuela ushered over the next mother and child and began translating his questions carefully. Manuela was another source of regret. All their efforts seemed to have come to nothing. She'd leave tomorrow with her family. The Flanagan family had declared their intention of staying in touch with her, but how realistic was that?

A shadow fell across the shaft of sunlight from the open door. He looked up to see Brendan Flanagan hurrying toward him, a broad smile on his face.

"Jake, I have news." He glanced at Manuela and

then at the child, sitting in his mother's lap. "I won't interrupt, but once you're free, will you meet me in the back room?"

"Of course." Judging by Brendan's cheerful expression, this wasn't about the gossip that was circulating through the hospital. At least, he hoped not.

Brendan nodded and started across the room, stopping to talk to everyone he met. Their clients were used to the pastor by now, and they tried very politely not to smile at his fractured Spanish.

Jake smiled at Manuela. "It's a good thing I have you to translate for me, and not Pastor Brendan. He'd probably tell the mother to put the vitamins in her baby's ear."

Manuela managed a smile, but her sorrow still showed, like a cloud darkening the sun. The poor kid wanted an education so much, and she saw it slipping out of reach.

He'd like to believe she'd be able to go to school at the next migrant camp, but that seemed a futile wish. He'd like to encourage her, but he wouldn't be much good at that right now.

He glanced around while she gave the instructions to the young mother. "It looks as if we're about finished for the day. I'm going back to speak to Pastor Brendan. Will you clean up for me?"

"It is my pleasure," she said, patting the baby's head.

Those weren't just words, he knew. Manuela so obviously enjoyed every moment of her work at the clinic, even the routine cleaning that others might try to avoid.

I know I don't deserve any happy endings, but shouldn't Manuela have her chance?

He went quickly through the door to the back room

of the clinic, stopping short when he saw Terry. Brendan grinned at him. "Come on in. I've got some news that will knock your socks off."

"Just tell us." Terry fidgeted, not glancing toward him. "Stop teasing."

Brendan shook his head. "Don't you remember that patience is one of the fruits of the Spirit, kid?"

"It's not one I've managed to grow yet, so unless you want the proof of that—"

"Okay, okay." Brendan held up both hands, as if to fend her off. "Thanks to my lovely and talented wife, who did all the research, we've done the thing. Manuela can stay with Joe and Siobhan and attend school, at least until her family is ready to go back to Mexico."

Terry's face lit up like a Christmas tree, and she threw her arms around her cousin. "Brendan, I could kiss you. That's wonderful news. And tell Claire we really owe her for this."

"That is good news." He felt out of place in the midst of all this Flanagan family rejoicing. He hadn't contributed much to the cause except a few dollars out of his pocket. "Shall I bring Manuela in?"

"Let me do it." Terry darted past him. "I can't wait to see her face."

Brendan looked at him and shrugged. "Terry's the excitable one of the family. Can you tell?"

He nodded. Obviously Brendan didn't know that there was anything wrong between him and Terry, even though he felt as if the chill in the air was advertising it to the world.

Terry was back in a moment, propelling Manuela, who looked half-frightened.

"What is it? Have I done something wrong?"

"Of course not." Terry hugged her. "We just have good news." She nodded to Brendan.

"At least we think it is good news." Brendan's calm tone must have reassured Manuela. "If you want to, and if your parents agree, we've arranged for you to stay with Terry and her parents and go to school here. Would you like that?"

"Stay?" For a moment there was no expression at all on her face.

"Until your parents go back to Mexico, at least. What do you think?"

Her gaze sought out Jake's. "Dr. Jake? This is true?"

"Pastor Brendan has made all the arrangements. It's true."

Maybe, when she heard it from him, she thought it was safe to believe. The expression on her face was sunshine, breaking through to light a cloudy day.

"I can stay," she repeated, swinging toward Terry and grabbing her arms. "I can stay!"

"You sure can." Terry enveloped her in a hug, all the love in that warm heart of hers shining in her eyes. Over Manuela's shoulder, her gaze met his. Met, and nearly knocked him off his feet.

Terry. His heart felt as if it was twisted in a vise. He wanted to believe she hadn't let him down. He hadn't realized until this moment how much he wanted to believe that.

Manuela wiped tears from her cheeks. "I must go and tell my parents. I must ask my father for permission." She hesitated. "I will finish cleaning up first."

"No, you won't." He smiled at her, forcing himself

to look at her, not Terry. "We can muddle through without you this once. Go."

She nodded, smiling through her tears, and darted toward the door.

He didn't dare look at Terry, because he didn't know what she might read in his eyes. Or what he might read in hers.

At least, if nothing else, Manuela was getting her happy ending.

When Jake finally finished congratulating Brendan and went back into the clinic's work area, Terry sagged against the nearest counter. She hadn't realized how hard it would be to go on pretending everything was fine when Jake was around.

She caught Brendan looking at her and straightened. "I guess I'd better get back to work."

"That can wait a minute." Brendan came to lean against the counter next to her, putting his arm across her shoulders. "Come on, give. What's wrong between you and Jake?"

She pressed her fingers against her forehead, trying to will away the dull ache that throbbed at her temples. "It shows, huh?"

"It does to me." His grasp tightened. "Can I help?"

"I don't think anyone can fix this one." She managed a ghost of a smile. "Even me. Jake believes I broke a confidence."

"Well, if he believes that, he doesn't know you very well, does he?"

"I thought he did." Her voice quivered, and she tried to swallow the lump in her throat.

"I'm sorry, Ter. I wish I could make it better."

She nodded. "It's just—I've been trying to follow God's leading. It's hard to understand why things work out the way they do sometimes."

"I know." His voice roughened, and he pressed a light kiss against her temple. "I know."

A pang of regret went through her. Brendan, of all people, knew how that was. He and Claire had been trying for a baby since their wedding, and that prayer hadn't been answered.

"So what do you do when you don't see any chance that things are going to turn out the way you hoped and prayed?"

"I guess I just keep trying to run the race." His smile flickered. "Here comes the minister, quoting scripture. 'Since we are surrounded by so great a cloud of witnesses, let us lay aside every weight, and the sin which so easily ensnares us, and let us run with endurance the race that is set before us.' Some days that's just more of a challenge than others. And some days I just want to lie down by the side of the track."

She had to smile at the wry tone. "Right." She went on tiptoe to kiss his cheek. "I knew there was some good reason we have a minister in the family. Thanks, Bren."

"Any time."

She took a deep breath. Okay, on to the next thing. She marched back out to the clinic.

The last few stragglers had gone through while she'd been in the back, and the remaining volunteers were packing up, getting ready to leave. She felt a pang of regret. Most of the workers would be on their way south tomorrow, and the clinic would remain open only three days a week to serve those who stayed. The project was drawing to a close. They'd done a good job, and seeing it end was bittersweet.

Gradually, the volunteers filed out, followed by Brendan, until only she and Jake were left.

She cleared her throat. "There's not much else to do. I can handle it, if you want to leave. I'm staying until Manuela comes back anyway, so we can talk about getting her moved to the house."

He nodded, sliding some forms into the file cabinet, but he didn't seem in any hurry to leave. "That's a nice thing your folks are doing."

"It's always open house at the Flanagans. I've gotten used to coming home and finding that someone has moved in for a while." She smiled. "The latest is my cousin Fiona. Dad's still protesting that one, but Mom's already invited her to come."

"It'll be good for Manuela, having you around as a role model."

That startled her. She swung to face him. "If I'd really spread rumors about you, I'd hardly be a good role model for anyone, would I?"

He just stared at her, the width of the room between them. "Did you?"

"No." Did he believe her? And would it make any difference if he did?

His brows drew together. "I want to accept that. It's just that I don't see how anyone else could know."

Believe me, Jake. For your sake, if not for mine. "You've said yourself what a small world the medical community is, and Philadelphia isn't that far away. Is it so hard to believe that someone else in Suffolk might have connections there?"

He considered that for a long moment, his eyes grave. "You know who it is, don't you?"

"I can't answer that without breaking someone else's confidence."

His mouth tightened, but finally he nodded. "Fair enough. I guess I owe you an apology. When I saw you with Manuela—well, I just knew you didn't have it in you to do something like that. I should have known the moment I heard about it. I'm sorry, Terry. That was a poor repayment for everything you've done."

She let out a breath she hadn't realized she'd been holding. It took a struggle to keep her voice even, but she didn't want him to guess at the happiness that bubbled through her. "It's all right. I'm just glad we're friends again."

A smile lit his grave expression. "Same here. There's something I'd like to tell you." He turned away, as if he didn't want to look at her when he said the words. "I'm thinking of accepting my father's offer and going back to Boston."

At some level, she'd thought she was prepared for that. But she wasn't. It was slicing her heart into little pieces. She swallowed, trying to loosen tight muscles enough to speak. "Whatever you decide, I wish you—"

Her words cut off when the screen door slammed. Manuela stood there, breathing hard, hand pressed to her diaphragm.

"Manuela? What is it? What's wrong?" Apprehension clawed at her.

"My father." Manuela gasped the words. "I can't. My father won't allow it. He won't let me stay."

"Oh, Manuela." Her heart twisted as she put her arm around the girl's shoulders. Manuela shook with suppressed sobs. "I'm so sorry. Why doesn't he want to? Maybe if we talked to him, it would make a difference."

Manuela shook her head, crying too much to say anything coherent. Terry looked at Jake over the girl's bent head, seeing the sorrow there.

"We did it all wrong," she said. "We should have gone to the family first. We have to go and talk to him."

Jake took Manuela by the shoulders. "Crying isn't going to help." His tone was brisk. "Let's talk this over and see what we can do."

Terry glared at him. That was taking detachment a little too far, wasn't it? Still, it seemed to be working. Manuela choked back her sobs and wiped her cheeks with her hands, looking at Jake obediently.

"That's better." He grabbed a tissue from the box on the desk and handed it to her. "Now, let's figure out what we should do. Did your father give any reason for telling you no?"

Manuela sniffed a little. "He doesn't trust outsiders. He thinks we'll only be safe if we're with him."

"Well, maybe we can find a way of reassuring him."

"We'll go over right now—" Terry began, but Jake shook his head at her.

"This may work out better if we have someone else to translate for us. I'll see if I can reach Maria Esteban." He pulled out his cell phone and began to flip through the list of volunteers that was posted over the desk.

It made sense, she supposed, to recruit the volunteer

nurse who spoke fluent Spanish, but she didn't want to wait. The need to do something pulsed through her. She couldn't let Manuela's chance slip away if there was anything she could do.

She tried to comfort the girl while listening to Jake's side of a short conversation. He flipped the phone closed, frowning a little.

"Maria will be glad to help, but she doesn't have transportation. I'll have to run into town and get her. Maybe you should come along."

She suspected he was thinking that he didn't want her to do anything rash. "I'll walk over with Manuela and meet you at the camp. All right?"

Jake looked a little doubtful, but he nodded. He gave Manuela an encouraging smile. "Don't give up yet. We may still be able to work this out."

He turned and went quickly out of the clinic to his car. Manuela looked as if she'd begin to cry again once he was gone, so Terry handed her a stack of sheets. "Put these in the closet for me, please. I'll just lock the medication in my car and then we'll go."

There were a few more things to do, but she could deal with them later. She shoved the drug box into her trunk for safety and slipped her cell phone in her pocket.

"Okay. Let's go."

Manuela followed her silently toward the path that skirted the hillside, leading toward the housing facility. It was so quiet here; no one would guess that on the far side of the rounded, wooded mountain, there was a busy interstate, leading out to the wider world. Sometimes she felt as if they were cocooned in their little world.

If she didn't do something, Manuela would be

leaving this world, going on to the unknown—to another migrant camp where she might or might not find a welcome.

Are we wrong, Lord, to try and keep her here for a while? I know it might be hard for her to be away from her family, but she has such a thirst for knowledge. It seems wrong to deny her this chance.

She glanced at the girl. Manuela walked with her head down, her gaze fixed on her feet. All of her bright confidence seemed to have fled, leaving her lost and resigned to whatever life might hand her.

"It's going to be all right." She spoke as much to reassure herself as Manuela. "You'll see."

Manuela just shook her head, her black braids swinging.

The poor kid—what must she be feeling? They'd held out to her the promise of a path toward the education she longed for, and now that hope had been dashed.

They emerged from the trees and approached the cement block buildings. A quick glance showed Terry that Jake and the translator hadn't arrived yet, but Mel Jordan, the crew chief, swung around at their approach, staring at them with narrowed eyes.

"What are you doing here?" He shot a look from her to Manuela. "Haven't you caused enough trouble?"

Temper, temper. Her mother was always telling her she had to learn to control herself. She forced a smile to her face. "I'm here to talk with Manuela's parents."

"They don't want to talk to you. They don't like interfering outsiders."

"I'll let them tell me that." She moved to go around him, but he stepped into her path.

She'd dealt with recalcitrant patients and violent drunks on duty. She wouldn't be intimidated by him. "Please get out of my way."

"How are you going to make me?"

The sound of a car engine answered him. Terry looked up to see Jake's car pulling into the graveled lot in front of the dorms, and a wave of relief went through her.

"I don't think I'll have to."

Jordan shot a balked, annoyed look at the car and then turned and stalked away.

Jake got out and came toward her, followed by Maria. "Trouble?" He frowned, as if to say he couldn't trust her alone for more than a minute at a time.

"Not now." She smiled at the nurse. "Thanks for coming out, Maria."

"My pleasure." Maria shoved a lock of dark hair back from her face. She must have come straight from work, because she wore hospital scrubs. "Manuela is a dear. I'm happy to help."

"Let's get this done," Jake said briskly. "Manuela, will you come in with us?"

Manuela shook her head, taking a step back. "My father—he would not change his mind in front of me."

"Okay." Terry squeezed her hand, understanding. Manuela's culture was different from that of the typical American teenager.

Terry followed Jake and Maria into the large, square room, which had been filled with the aroma of cooking the last time she'd been here. Today it looked dusty and deserted. Deserted, except for one person—Manuela's father sat at one of the rickety wooden tables, as if waiting for them.

Terry took a breath, suddenly shaky. *Please, Lord.*

Jake took the lead, and she was happy to let him. With Maria translating, he told Mr. Ortiz what their plans were—how happy they'd be to have Manuela stay with them so she could go to school. That they'd bring her to meet them when it was time for the family to return to Mexico. That they'd make sure she was safe and happy.

And she knew it was no good. She might not understand the words Maria spoke to him, but she understood his response. No. No matter what Maria said to him, the answer was the same. No.

Maria finally turned back to them, shaking her head. "I'm sorry. It's no good. He doesn't trust us, and I suppose he can't be blamed for that. He says Manuela is needed to help her mother. He fears that if she stays, even for a couple of months, she won't want to go back."

Manuela's father rose, shoving his chair back. His face stoic, he turned and stalked into the back room.

"That's it then." Jake's face was bleak. "We'd better tell Manuela."

"What's wrong with you? We can't give up that easily." Her fists clenched. Didn't Jake see how important this was?

"There's nothing we can do." It almost sounded as if he pitied her. "We've tried everything possible."

"Not everything." Her mind scrambled to come up with some other solution. "Maybe if we took them to see my parents, he'd see that we don't mean any harm. Or maybe Mr. Dixon could speak to him. He might listen to him."

"No." The pity was eaten up by what sounded like frustration. "Give it up, Terry. It's over, and you'll only make it harder for Manuela if you keep holding out false hope."

She wanted to argue, but his words hit home. Her throat tightened. "I'm afraid we've already done that."

He gripped her shoulder for a moment, his touch conveying sympathy and support. "Do you want me to tell her?"

"No. I will." This had been her idea. She'd have to accept the responsibility for this failure.

"I have to drive Maria back to town. Are you going to be all right?"

She nodded, her throat too tight to speak. Manuela would leave, to be lost in the stream of migrant workers. And it looked as if Jake would leave, too. She was going to be all right, but she'd be a long time filling the hole they'd left in her heart.

She followed Jake and Maria outside and watched while they drove away. Then she looked around for Manuela.

There was no sight of her, but the sound of childish voices led her around the side of the building. Juan, Manuela's little brother, was playing with a couple of older children.

She squatted next to him. "Hey, Juan. Where's Manuela?" The boy's English had improved immensely in the past few weeks. Surely he could understand that.

For a moment, Juan's face was stolid, as expressionless as his father's had been, as if he were a little old man, inured to the blows of life. Then his face puckered.

"She go." He pointed toward the narrow logging road that led over the mountain, towards the interstate. "She go up there when she wants to be by herself." His face puckered. "I want her to come back."

Chapter Fifteen

She wanted her to come back, too. Terry's heart hurt at the thought of the girl alone someplace in the woods, crying. "When Dr. Jake comes back, tell him where I went. Okay?" She gestured to herself and to the path, hoping he understood. Then she started up the trail.

She glanced at her watch. Nearly four. At least, in early September, she wasn't going to run out of daylight anytime soon. She hadn't attempted to find out from Juan how long Manuela had been gone. The little boy's English wouldn't have been up to that. In any event, they hadn't spent more than twenty minutes with Mr. Ortiz.

Poor Manuela. She must have guessed how their interview with her father would go. So she was running off and hiding, like an injured animal. She was only sixteen and acting on emotion, not common sense. She depended on the adults in her life for that, and they seemed to be letting her down.

Please, Lord. Manuela is out there alone, and I have to reach her. Please, lead me to her, and give me the right words to say to her when I find her.

The hill grew steeper, and the logging road disintegrated to a shallow wash filled with last year's dead leaves. Manuela had gone up here before. There should be nothing to worry about, but fear was chilling her, as if to warn her.

The signal strength flickered from one bar to none. She punched in the number, but it went straight to Jake's voice mail. Static crackled in her ear.

"Manuela's disappeared. Juan says she goes up into the woods to be alone. I've gone after her." She hesitated, not wanting to sound irrational. "Please come. I need you."

She flipped the phone closed, feeling marginally better, and focused on forcing her aching legs up the trail. Afternoon sunlight, slanting through the trees, gave the woods an almost golden glow. The sumac bushes that grew along the trail had already donned their fall color. Autumn was on its way, summer slipping imperceptibly away.

She stopped, pressing her hand against her side, catching her breath. She listened, but no sound broke the silence except the faint twittering of birds. It couldn't be far to the crest of the ridge. Surely Manuela wouldn't go farther than that.

"Manuela! Manuela, can you hear me? It's Terry."

Nothing. Maybe she'd heard and didn't want to answer. She probably thought Terry had already failed her.

The taste of that failure filled Terry's mouth. Manuela was right. Terry had held out a promise to her that she hadn't been able to fulfill.

Please, Father. I want so much to make up for this. Let me find a way to help her now.

It was harder and harder to climb. Terry scrambled to

the slight ridge along the side of the log drag. The footing was firmer there, but rocky and treacherous with the tangle of tree roots that forced their way to the surface.

She slowed for a moment, trying to orient herself. Ahead was the top of the ridge. It would slope down fairly quickly on the other side. She couldn't believe Manuela would go that far.

"Manuela! Come on, if you can hear me, let me know." Again nothing. Maybe Manuela had gone back to the camp already, and she was foolishly overreacting.

Terry's breath caught. Was that the cry of a bird? It almost sounded—

"Help! Help me!"

Manuela! Terry charged toward the sound, heart thumping. "Manuela, where are you? I'm coming. Keep calling out."

"Help…"

The voice seemed fainter, but it gave Terry enough direction. She cut to the right, scrambling as fast as she could up the increasingly rocky slope. Another wordless sob sent her hurtling ahead.

She stopped, heart pounding, grabbing the rough trunk of a hemlock tree. Beyond the tree, a ravine cut through the ridge top, as sharp as a knife slice. Clutching the tree, she leaned forward, scanning the steep tumble of rocks and gravel. A few small trees grew out at odd angles from the wall of the ravine.

At the bottom—her breath caught. At the bottom lay a small crumpled figure. The instinct that sent her here was true.

"Manuela, it's all right. I'm coming." *Please, God. Let her be all right.*

She forced herself to concentrate. She had to look at this as a professional, as if the victim were a stranger, not a girl she'd come to care for. Anything else invited hasty decisions and increased the chance of making a mistake.

She yanked out her cell phone, but as soon as she glanced at it, she knew she was on her own. No signal. No help. Just her skill and caring.

Quickly she assessed the scene. If she attempted to climb down directly above the girl, she'd risk sending a shower of rocks and gravel right down on her. She'd have to take a slower, more roundabout route.

"Manuela, I'm on my way down. How are you? Talk to me." Was she conscious? She had to get to her, stabilize her, then find some way of getting help.

A low moan was the only answer. Adrenaline pumping, Terry hurried her pace—scramble down a few feet, stop and assess the next step, then go on. She had no equipment with her, just her hands and her knowledge.

"Come on, Manuela, talk to me."

She was close enough to see the twisted way the girl sprawled. That leg was probably fractured.

"It hurts."

Relief spread through her at the sound of Manuela's voice. Praise God, she wasn't unconscious.

"I know it hurts, honey." She slid down the last few feet, picking up an assortment of scrapes and scratches, and raced across the rough ground to drop to her knees next to the girl. "You're going to be okay. I'm here now."

Manuela didn't attempt to move, but her gaze focused on Terry's face and clung there. "You came."

"Of course I came."

She kept her voice calm even as her heart twisted.

Quickly she assessed the damage. No bleeding, and Manuela was conscious, but her breathing was shallow, her pulse rapid. Her first instinct was to immobilize the spine, but she had nothing to work with.

"Tell me where it hurts."

"My leg." Manuela gasped the words. "And my chest." She gestured slightly toward her ribs on the right side.

"How about your head?"

"It's okay."

She moved her hands lightly over the small body, feeling helpless without her usual equipment. Still, it was her knowledge and skill Manuela needed now. The right leg was definitely fractured, but she was more concerned with the ribs. Probably a fracture there, as well, and in a place where it could so easily puncture a lung.

She touched the girl's face gently. "You're going to be all right. Believe me. I'm going to immobilize your leg, and then I'll have to go for help."

Manuela's eyes widened, and she grasped Terry's arm. "Don't leave me."

"Honey, I wouldn't if I had any choice. But I need help getting you out of here safely, and my cell phone isn't working this deep in the woods. There's nothing else to do. You trust me, don't you?"

The girl's gaze clung to hers. Slowly, she nodded.

Am I doing the right thing? Please, Lord, show me. I don't want to leave her alone, but I don't see what else I can do.

"Okay, then." She squeezed Manuela's hand. "All you have to do is stay perfectly still. Right?"

"Right." The ghost of a smile crossed her face.

Terry's heart clenched again. Manuela was a fighter. She wouldn't give up easily, no matter how hard the battle.

It took a few minutes to immobilize the girl as best she could, using broken branches and strips torn from the tail of her shirt. And all the while her brain was ticking away the moments from finding the victim to getting her to the hospital. Too many minutes. Manuela needed more care than she could provide in this situation.

From now on, Father, I'm not going anyplace without a decent first aid kit.

When she'd done everything she could, she hesitated for a moment, then bent and kissed Manuela's forehead. "Be a brave girl, and I'll be back before you know it. God be with you."

"And with you," Manuela whispered.

Terry had to force herself to let go. No choices, she reminded herself. Manuela needed help, and she had to bring it. It would take time to get a unit here, more time to maneuver a gurney into the ravine and out again. That had to be done while they still had daylight to work by.

Jake, I wish you were here.

She turned toward the hill and began to climb, as quickly as possible. Trying to climb away from the doubt that pursued her.

Was she doing the right thing? Had she exhausted every other option? Even when she knew she had no other choice, the habit of self-questioning had burned so deeply that she couldn't shake it off.

She grabbed a drooping branch of the hemlock and used it to pull herself up the last few yards. She hesitated, still hanging on, and looked down at Manuela. The girl looked so small, lying there. Pain gripped her heart.

Lord, this is my fault. If I hadn't encouraged her, it never would have happened. She'd be safe with her family.

She took a breath, pinned a smile to her face, and waved down at the girl. Regrets couldn't help Manuela now. Only action could.

"Remember, stay very still. I'll be back before you know it."

Manuela wiggled her fingers.

That was the image she'd carry with her. Terry turned and scrambled down toward the trail. Not images of failure. The image of a brave girl who relied on her. Trusted her. She wouldn't let her down.

She slithered down the last few yards of rocky slope and landed on the low ridge of ground that bordered the logging trail. Her feet found balance and she began to hurry, afraid to run where the ground was still so rough. If she fell and became immobilized, who would help Manuela then?

You would fail her. That insidious voice whispered in the back of her mind. *You would fail again.*

She tried to ignore it, but the doubt began to creep through her. She hit a patch of dead leaves, slid and fetched up against the trunk of an oak tree, breathing hard and clutching it.

You're okay. She tried to still her frazzled nerves. *Don't think about how near you came to falling. Just do the job that is set in front of you.*

She scrambled down a few more yards, searching for solid ground beneath her feet. Once she reached that, she could begin to run. But her breath was coming in gasps, and her leg muscles had begun to shake from the exertion.

Please, Lord. Please. I have to get help.

The words Brendan had spoken earlier seemed to form in her mind, as if in answer to her frenzied prayer.

Since we are surrounded by so great a cloud of witnesses, let us lay aside every weight, and the sin which so easily ensnares us, and let us run with endurance the race that is set before us.

She knew, only too well, the weight of self-doubt that hampered her, and the sin of giving in to that, setting snares for her feet. But she was not alone. She was never truly alone. Calm flowed through her in a cleansing wave.

She took a breath, feeling the weight roll off her, and hastened her steps, gaining sureness with every stride. The ground became firmer under her feet, and she began to jog, then to run, the trees hurrying past as she kept her eyes on the goal and her mind on her Lord.

Down past the growth of pines and hemlocks that crowned the top of the hill, past the maples and oaks, the thick patches of rhododendron and mountain laurel, the sumacs lifted their bronze torches high as if to show her the way.

Her breath came hard now, but her legs felt strong. She could run all day if she had to. She could do it.

But she didn't have to, because there was Jake, coming up through the trees toward her. And, blessing of blessings, he carried her med kit with him.

He started to run when he saw her, and she slithered down through the fallen leaves to bump into him. He grabbed her, holding her securely.

"Did you find her? Is she all right?"

"She fell." She gasped out the words. "No head or spine

injury that I could detect, but a leg fracture and possible rib fractures. I stabilized as best I could, but we've got to get back to her. Thank God you brought the kit."

"You sounded so upset—it seemed like a good idea. If you go on down for help—"

"You might not find her without my help." If she'd lost consciousness. Terry didn't want to say the words, but Jake knew what she meant. She yanked out her cell phone and saw, to her relief, that she finally had a signal.

It took only seconds to call in the accident, setting the mechanism in motion for the rescue effort. They wouldn't be able to bring the unit up that logging trail, but the department had an ATV for situations just like this one.

"Straight up the logging trail toward the ridge. We'll mark the point at which you have to leave the trail." Her shirt was taking a beating, but she could sacrifice a little more. "Watch for a yellow streamer where you have to veer off to the right."

She ended the call, knowing she was ending contact with her lifeline. But it didn't seem to matter. Jake was with her, and the Lord was guiding both of them.

Jake leaned against a tree, catching his breath while Terry tied a strip of fabric from her shirt to the branch of a shrub overhanging the trail they'd been on. He felt like sliding right down to the ground, but Terry looked as if she could go on forever. And she'd already been up and down this mountainside. He'd admired her before, but never quite so much as he did at this moment.

If only —but what did he have to offer her? An uncertain future with a man who couldn't trust his own feelings?

"This way." Terry forged ahead.

He followed. All he could do now was concentrate on Manuela. Get her stabilized, get her to the hospital. That was all either of them could do.

Terry moved between two trees and suddenly seemed to disappear. Heart in his throat, he reached the trees and found her climbing down at an angle into a ravine he hadn't even guessed was there. She looked up, her gaze meeting his, and jerked her head toward the ravine floor.

Manuela. The girl lay very still, and he couldn't tell from here whether she was conscious or not. He slung the kit over his shoulder and started down in Terry's path.

"We can't go straight, or we'd sent rocks down on her." Terry moved as surely as if she did this every day. "Manuela, we're coming."

He heard the tension in her voice, felt it echo through him.

Father, I haven't asked much lately. I've felt so separated from You. Please, be with us now. Guide us to save this child.

Then he was too busy climbing to think of anything but getting down the steep slope in one piece. Finally he and Terry rushed to Manuela.

Her eyes flickered open. "You came," she whispered. "I knew." She stopped, gasping for breath. "Hurts."

He already had a stethoscope out, but he knew what he was going to find even before he listened. Decreased breath sounds on one side—just what he'd suspect with a pneumothorax.

His gaze met Terry's, and he nodded.

"What has happened?" Manuela gasped the words. "I can't breathe."

"It's okay, honey." Terry's voice was sure and soothing. She smoothed hair away from the girl's face. "You have a broken rib, and it's causing your lung to collapse. They'll be able to fix it when we get you to the hospital."

He shook his head, frustrated at the limited supplies at their command. "How long?" He looked at Terry. She was the expert at this aspect of care. "How long until the team reaches us, gets her out, gets back to the hospital?"

Her eyes darkened with fear. "Probably close to an hour for them to reach us. Another hour to get her out safely and get to the E.R."

"That's too long." He began to sift through the med kit, automatically double-checking what they had to work with. "We can't wait."

"You're going to put in a chest tube."

He lifted his eyebrows at her tone. "You don't agree?"

"It's not that." She lowered her voice. "What about the clinic rules? Morley will have a fit when he learns you've done a procedure like that out here."

For just a moment he hesitated. Some analytical part of his mind, that part of him that was like his father, weighed and measured the risks and benefits—not just to the patient, but to him and his career.

Then he looked at Terry, watching him, ready to do whatever he wanted to assist him. At Manuela, lying helpless, looking at him to take care of her.

There really wasn't anything to measure at all. A

sense of freedom washed over him. "We're doing it." He smiled at Manuela. "Hang on, sweetheart. We're not going to let you down."

Chapter Sixteen

Terry hesitated in the hallway outside the waiting room. Manuela's family was inside, waiting for word from the doctors who were treating her. It shouldn't be long. Manuela was going to be fine—she was sure of that. God had held her in His hand today.

By the time the rescue team had arrived, Jake had successfully inserted the chest tube. Manuela was breathing easier, and they'd splinted the leg and had her ready for transport. Terry had been so proud of the fire-fighters and paramedics as they'd brought the stretcher down into the ravine, loaded Manuela and taken her back up as gently as if they'd lifted fragile china.

Everything had gone exactly as it should. Still, she hesitated to face Manuela's parents. What must they think of her? It had been her interference that had brought Manuela to this place.

She couldn't be a coward about it. She'd go in and try to comfort them while they waited. Even from outside the door, she could hear the murmur of Maria's voice. The nurse had been with the Ortiz family, translating, from the moment she'd heard what happened.

The elevator doors at the end of the hall swished open. Perhaps Jake—

But it wasn't Jake who stepped off the elevator. It was Matthew Dixon.

She stared at him blankly. What was he doing here? Surely not checking on Manuela—he'd exhibited little enough caring for his workers to this point.

Dixon stalked down the hall to her and stopped, fixing her with that intimidating glare. "You're here, are you? I guessed you would be."

"I'm waiting to hear how Manuela is. They should be ready to take her to a room soon."

He nodded shortly. "Heard about it. Heard about how you're the one who found her, too. You did a fine job."

"Thank you." That was surprising praise from him.

"Something else I have to say to you." White brows drew down over his fierce blue eyes. "I didn't believe you. What you said about the housing. You want to know why I didn't believe you?"

She nodded.

"Because I put my son in charge of renovating the housing months before the crews arrived. I turned that over to him, along with a lot of other things that had to be done, after I had a bad turn with my heart back in the spring." His face was bleak and old. "Turns out I shouldn't have trusted him. My own son, and he was salting the money away for himself instead of using it the way I ordered."

"I'm so sorry." But not, she realized, totally surprised at some level. Maybe she'd always recognized something lacking in Andy's character. She put her hand on Dixon's arm. "I really am. If there's anything I can do—"

He covered her hand with his. "Nothing. I made a mistake, keeping Andy here, thinking he'd want to take over the operation once I couldn't run it anymore. It'll be better for him to be on his own for a while. Maybe give him time to do some growing up." He fixed a pleading gaze on her. "That's what he needs, don't you think?"

Her heart hurt for him. Maybe he had made mistakes in raising his son, but he didn't deserve this betrayal. "You're probably right." She patted his hand. "Do you want to go in with me to see Manuela's parents?"

He hesitated for an instant and then squared his shoulders, nodding. She knew exactly how reluctant and guilty he felt, because she felt the same. Together they approached the waiting room.

Mr. and Mrs. Ortiz looked up simultaneously when they appeared, faces questioning. Juan sat on a chair in the corner, completely absorbed in the cartoon program someone had put on the video player for him.

"No news yet," Terry said quickly. "Maria, please assure them that she was stable when we brought her in."

"I already have, but I will again." Maria spoke quickly to the parents.

Terry cleared her throat. "There's something else I have to say, if you'll translate for me. I'm so very sorry. I realize my responsibility in all this. It was my idea to offer Manuela the opportunity to stay for a few months to attend school. I didn't realize her family would refuse, or how badly Manuela would take it—"

"*¿Que?*" Manuela's mother interrupted the soft flow

of Maria's voice. She turned on her husband, letting loose a torrent of words that battered at him. He began shaking his head, obviously trying to explain something, but she didn't seem to want to hear it.

Maria blinked, looking from the agitated parents to Terry and Matthew Dixon. "Apparently, Mr. Ortiz never talked to his wife about your offer. She seems to have some pretty strong feelings about it herself. She wants Manuela to have her chance at a good education."

Hope flickered through Terry. If only something good could come out of this. *Please, God.*

Maria paused for a moment, listening to the rapid exchanges between the parents. "He's arguing that it's not safe to leave a young girl here with strangers, no matter how nice they may seem."

"Wait one minute." Matthew Dixon stalked across the waiting room and came to a halt in front of the upset parents. "This girl that's hurt is the one you talked to me about?"

Terry nodded. The situation had spun out of her control. She could only watch and wonder where it would go next.

"You." He barked the word at Maria. "Tell them that I have a permanent job for them, if they want to stay. A decent place to live, too. I could use both of them, if Mrs. Ortiz is willing to look after the house and Mr. Ortiz wants farm work. Tell them." His face tightened. "I've got a bit of making up to do. That's a good first step, if they agree."

Terry held her breath, but she didn't have to wait until Maria had translated their answer to know what it was. The expressions on their faces told her only too clearly. They would stay. Manuela would have her happy ending.

She blinked back tears. Manuela deserved it, and she wouldn't allow even a whimper of self-pity to ask why she couldn't have the same.

Jake paused in the doorway to the patient room. Manuela, leg encased in plaster, lay propped up in bed, still on oxygen, but looking much better. Her skin had not quite returned to its rosy glow. Still, the contented smile that touched her lips and the happiness in her eyes more than made up for that.

Her parents sat on either side of her bed, talking to her softly. Terry was bending over Juan, showing him a book, but she looked up as if she knew he was there.

She rose quickly, coming toward him. "Come in, please. You're the hero of the hour. I know Manuela's parents want to thank you."

"You're the one they should thank." He pressed her hand, longing to tell her what he felt, but not daring to venture there. "You're the one who ran up and down that mountainside twice today. Feeling a little sore?"

"By tomorrow I will." She grimaced. "But don't you dare tell anyone I admitted it. Paramedics are supposed to be tough."

"I wouldn't dream of it."

Tough? Well, Terry was tough in the professional way she needed to be, but in every other way she was more tender and warmhearted than anyone he'd ever met. And he couldn't tell her so.

The parents, roused by their soft conversation, came toward him, beaming, their gratitude overflowing in words he couldn't understand. Still, they didn't need translation, did they?

He nodded, smiled and felt relieved when Terry's parents, her sister, Mary Kate and Pastor Brendan came in. Their arrival took the pressure off him—the pressure to accept gratitude for something he'd actually hesitated to do.

"They don't understand the risk you took." Terry's soft words reminded him that she seemed to have developed the ability to sense his thoughts.

He managed a smile and resisted the impulse to pull her against him and bury his face in her bright hair. "They don't ever need to know." He shrugged. "As for the risk—well, it may have made my decision for me, in a way."

Something that could have been pain darkened her eyes. "That's not fair. Surely you're not going to let Mr. Morley force you out for doing something you know was medically necessary."

Her caring moved him more than he could say. "Don't make a crusade out of me, Terry. I don't need rescuing." Quickly, before he could let her see too much, he moved out into the hall. "Tell Manuela I'll stop back to see her before she goes to sleep."

She nodded, accepting the rebuff, and turned back to the group around the bed.

He started down the hallway, not sure where he was going, just away from Terry. Around the first corner, he saw the hospital administrator, William Morley, coming straight toward him, purpose in every step.

So here it came, the end to his time in Suffolk. Now that he faced losing it, he recognized how much he had come to love this place, this job, these people. It wasn't just Terry, despite her importance to him.

This work was satisfying in a way that neurosurgery had never been. That had been nerve-racking, challenging, a personal triumph when he succeeded. But here— here he focused on the people—both the patients and the team. He loved this. And he was going to lose it.

"Dr. Landsdowne." Morley's tone didn't leave much doubt as to his agenda. "I can hardly believe what I've been told. You deliberately flouted the rules we set down for the clinic. I would not have believed it of you."

The self-righteousness in the man's tone set his teeth on edge. He'd had some brief thought of apologizing, of trying to justify what he'd done, of promising never to break the rules again, but that wouldn't be true to himself or to what God demanded of him.

"What wouldn't you believe, Mr. Morley? That I would put the patient's welfare above your petty regulations?"

Morley went red, then white. "Petty? You'll see how petty my regulations are. You've broken hospital rules, doctor, and your contract is hereby terminated."

"Well, now, what's all this?" Sam Getz's booming voice exploded the tension in the hallway into a million pieces. "Who's talking about termination?"

Morley stiffened. "This isn't the place to have this discussion."

"Seems to me you're the one who started it here." Getz's gaze had a hint of steel.

"Dr. Landsdowne has broken the rules that were clearly established and agreed upon for the clinic's operation, undertaking a risky procedure out in the woods, setting the hospital up for the possibility of a lawsuit—"

"Nonsense!"

The edge in Getz's voice sent Morley back a step.

"Really, Dr. Getz, I think you'll allow that hospital administration is my province."

"Supervising medical staff is mine, and I wouldn't give a nickel for any doctor who'd let rules come before saving a child's life." Ignoring the administrator, Dr. Getz focused on Jake. "I don't see any need in prolonging this probationary period. You're the man for the job here, and I've got the votes on the board to make it official. What do you say?"

"Yes." *Thank You, Lord.* "I say yes."

Terry was aware of Jake the instant he came in the patient's room. She'd lingered after the others had gone. Because she wanted to see him again? Probably.

He stopped just inside the door, letting it swing behind him. She slid off the faux leather chair and went to him, her sneakers making little sound on the tile floor.

"She's asleep," she whispered. "Her mother is coming back after she gets Juan to bed, so I thought I'd stay for a while."

"Taking care of other people, as always."

"I guess so." In the illumination provided by the night-light on Manuela's bed, she could see his face, but she wasn't sure of the expression in his eyes. "Is anything—did something happen?" Maybe she didn't have the right to ask, but she had to.

"Everything has happened." He shook his head. "I can hardly believe it. Morley was actually in the middle of firing me when Dr. Getz walked up and offered me the job permanently. Said he wouldn't give a nickel for a doctor who'd put rules before a child's life."

Happiness rippled through her. For him, she told herself. Not for her. "I'm so glad. I can just hear Sam Getz saying that. But what about your father, and the residency he arranged for you? I thought that was what you wanted."

"Maybe it was, once." In the dimness, his expression was inward, as if he still tried to understand himself. "You know, despite what happened between my father and me, I was still trying to apply his standards to my life. Trying to be the impersonal surgeon who never gets emotionally involved. Can you believe that?"

If Jake saw that, he'd come a long way. "I guess we're all affected by what our parents think."

"Don't get me wrong. I'm glad we're at least speaking to each other again, even if we'll never have the kind of relationship you have with your folks." He smiled suddenly, his face lighting. "But that's not the kind of doctor I want to be. What I've been doing here has been far more satisfying than that residency could ever be. This is what God intended for me all along."

Her heart was thudding so loudly it was a wonder he couldn't hear it. "That's wonderful. For you and for the patients you'll care for here."

"Just the patients?" His voice went very soft, and he brushed her cheek with his fingertips. "What about you, Terry? You must know how I feel. I'm not going to let my father's standards rule my personal life, either. Are you willing to give our love a chance?"

Now her heart was too full to allow for speech. She looked into his face, seeing the barriers swept away, the love shining unguarded in his eyes.

"Yes. Oh, yes." She stepped forward, feeling his arms close around her.

She didn't have to struggle any longer, constantly worrying about whether she'd done her best. She just had to do what she'd done out in the woods when Manuela's life was at stake—run the race God had set out for her, relying on Him, thankful that God had given her Jake to run life's race with her.

* * * * *

Dear Reader,

Thank you for picking up this latest book in the story of the Flanagan family. I hope you enjoyed visiting with old friends and meeting new ones.

I knew Terry should have a story of her own since the moment she walked onto the pages of *Hero in Her Heart,* and I'm glad she finally has the chance. It was difficult to find the right hero for her, but I think Jake Landsdowne fills the bill. Someone as strong as she is needed an equally strong hero!

The plight of migrant farm workers in this country is a very real one, as they are often totally dependent on the crew chiefs who bring them in—a situation ripe for exploitation. Churches have been at the forefront of ensuring decent treatment for them, as Pastor Brendan's church does in this story.

I hope you'll let me know how you felt about this story. I'd love to hear from you, and you can write to me at Steeple Hill Books, 233 Broadway, Suite 1001, New York, NY 10279, e-mail me at marta@martaperry.com or visit me on the Web at www.martaperry.com. Please come back for the next Flanagan story, *Restless Hearts,* coming in March 2007.

Blessings,

Marta Perry

And now, turn the page for a sneak preview of
RESTLESS HEARTS by Marta Perry.
On sale in March 2007
from Steeple Hill Love Inspired.

Chapter One

She was lost in the wilds of Pennsylvania. Fiona Flanagan peered through her windshield, trying to decipher which of the narrow roads the tilted signpost pointed to. Maybe this wasn't really the wilds, since the only living creature she'd encountered in the last fifteen minutes was the brown-and-white cow that stared mournfully at her from its pasture next to the road.

Clearly the cow wasn't going to help. She frowned down at the map drawn by one of her numerous Flanagan cousins, and decided that squiggly line probably meant she should turn right.

She could always phone her cousin Gabe, but she shrank from having to admit she couldn't follow a few simple directions. Both he and his wife had volunteered to drive her or to get one of his siblings to drive her, but she'd insisted she could do this herself.

The truth was that she'd spent the past two weeks feeling overwhelmed by the open friendliness offered by these relatives she'd never met before. She'd spent so many years feeling like an outsider in her father's house that she didn't know how to take this quick acceptance.

The pastures on either side of the road gave way to fields of cornstalks, yellow and brown in October. Maybe that was a sign that she was approaching civilization. Or not. She could find her way around her native San Francisco blindfolded, but the Pennsylvania countryside was another story.

The road rounded a bend and there, quite suddenly, was a cluster of houses and buildings that had to be the elusive hamlet she'd been seeking. Crossroads, the village was called, and it literally was a crossroads, a collection of dwellings grown up around the point at which two of the narrow blacktop roads crossed.

Relieved, she slowed the car, searching for something that might be a For Sale sign. The real estate agent with whom she'd begun her search had deserted her when he couldn't interest her in any of the sterile, bland, modern buildings he'd shown her on the outskirts of the busy, small city of Suffolk. But she didn't want suburban, she wanted the country. She had a vision of her practice as a nurse-midwife in a small community where she'd find a place to call home.

Through the gathering dusk she could see the glow of house lights in the next block. But where she was in the village, the few businesses were already closed. She drove by a one-pump service station, open, and a miniscule post office, closed. The Penn Dutch Diner had a few lights on, but only five cars graced its parking lot.

The Crossroads General Store, also closed, sat comfortably on her right, boasting a display of harnesses and tack in one window and an arrangement of what had to be genuine Amish quilts in the other. And there, next to it, was the sign she'd searched for: For Sale.

She drew up in front of the house. It had probably once been a charming Victorian, but now it sagged sadly, as if ashamed of such signs of neglect as cracked windows and peeling paint. But it had a wide, welcoming front porch, with windows on either side of the door, and a second floor that could become a cozy apartment above her practice.

For the first time in days of searching, excitement bubbled along her nerves. This might be it. If she squinted, she could picture the porch bright with autumn flowers in window boxes, a calico cat curled in the seat of a wicker rocker, and a neat brass plate beside the front door: Fiona Flanagan, Nurse-Midwife.

Home. The word echoed in her mind, setting up a sweet resonance. Home.

She slid out of the car, taking the penlight from her bag. Tomorrow she could get the key from the reluctant agent, but she'd at least get a glimpse inside in the meantime. She hurried up the three steps to the porch, avoiding a nasty gap in the boards, and approached the window on the left.

The dirt on the window combined with the feeble gleam of the penlight to thwart her ability to see inside. She rubbed furiously at the glass with a tissue. At a minimum she needed a waiting room, office, and exam room, and if—

"What do you think you're doing?" A gruff voice barked out the question, and the beam of a powerful light hit her like a blow, freezing her in place. "Well? Turn around and let me see you."

Heart thudding, she turned slowly, the penlight falling from sudden nerveless fingers. "I was just l-looking."

Great. She sounded guilty even to herself.

The tall, broad silhouette loomed to enormous proportions with the torch light in her eyes. She caught a glimpse of some metallic official insignia on the car that was pulled up in front of hers.

The man must have realized that the light was blinding her because he lowered the beam fractionally. "Come down off the porch."

She scrambled for the wandering penlight, grabbed it, and hurried down the steps to the street, trying to pull herself together. Really, she was overreacting. The man couldn't be as big and menacing as she was imagining.

But at ground level with him, she realized that her imagination wasn't really that far off. He must have stood well over six feet, with a solid bulk that suggested he was as immovable as one of the nearby hills. In the dim light, she made out a craggy face that looked as if it had been carved from rock. A badge glinted on his chest.

She rushed to explain. "Really, I didn't mean any harm. I understand this building is for sale, and I just wanted to have a quick look. I can come back tomorrow with the real estate agent."

She turned toward her car. Somehow, without giving the impression that the mountain had moved, the man managed to be between her and the vehicle.

Her heart began to pound against her ribs. She was alone in a strange place, with a man who was equally strange, and her cell phone was in her handbag, which lay unhelpfully on the front seat of the car she couldn't reach.

"Not so fast," he rumbled. "Let's see some identification, please."

At least she thought he said please—that slow rumble was a little difficult to distinguish. She could make out the insignia on his badge now, and her heart sank.

Crossroads Township Police. Why couldn't she have fallen into the hands of a nice, professional State Trooper, instead of a village cop who probably had an innate suspicion of strangers?

"My driver's license is in my car," she pointed out.

Wordlessly, he stood back for her to pass him and then followed her closely enough to open the door before she could reach the handle. She grabbed her wallet, pulling out the California driver's license and handing it to him.

"California." He seemed to pronounce all of the syllables separately.

"Yes, California." Nerves edged her voice. "Is that a problem, Officer?"

She snapped her mouth shut before she could say anything else. Don't make him angry. Never argue with a man who's wearing a large badge on his chest.

"Could be."

She blinked. She almost thought there was a thread of humor in the words.

He handed the ID back. "What brings you to Crossroads Township, Ms. Flanagan?"

"I'm looking for a house to buy. Someone from the real estate office mentioned this place. I got a little lost, or I'd have been here earlier."

She shifted her weight uneasily from one foot to the other as she said the words. That steady stare made her nervous. He couldn't really detain her for looking in a window, could he?

She looked up, considering saying that, and reconsidered at the sight of a pair of intense blue eyes in a stolid face made up entirely of planes. Don't say anything to antagonize him.

"I see." He invested the two words with a world of doubt. "You have anyone locally who can vouch for you?"

Finally she realized what she should have said sooner. Of course she had someone to vouch for her. She had a whole raft of cousins. Family. Not a word that usually had much warmth for her, but maybe now—

QUESTIONS FOR DISCUSSION

1. What qualities in Terry make her a good paramedic? Do you think she could be as effective without those innate qualities?

2. Jake feels as if this position is his last chance. How do you feel about his need to succeed? Do you approve of everything he does to achieve that?

3. Terry says to Manuela, "Once you've learned something, nobody can take that away. It will go with you wherever you are." Have you found that to be true in your life? How?

4. Terry finds she's envious that Jake thought of a way to help Manuela that she didn't. How have you shown similar feelings? In what circumstances?

5. Siobhan quotes the verse that says we are called for the good works God has already prepared for us. How have you found yourself led to the people and situations God has prepared for you?

6. Jake says he thought he was doing God's will in Africa, but then he contracted malaria and had to be sent home. How did God work in Jake's life in spite of that? How has God surprised you with the way in which He has used you?

7. As long as Jake couldn't forgive himself, he couldn't accept God's forgiveness. Why do you think forgiveness is such a difficult issue for so many Christians?

8. When she thinks of her future, Terry wants a God-centered, happy marriage. How important is it to put God at the center of a marriage? What happens when people don't?

9. Jake faces a dilemma—to do what he thinks is right at the risk of losing his job. How have you faced the difference between what the world expects and what God expects? How did you resolve it?

10. It can be difficult for people from another culture to adjust to a new society. Was staying the right decision for the Ortiz family? Why or why not?

Love Inspired®

PRECIOUS BLESSINGS

BY
JILLIAN HART

THE MCKASLIN CLAN

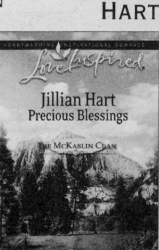

Steeple
Hill®

www.SteepleHill.com

LIPBJH

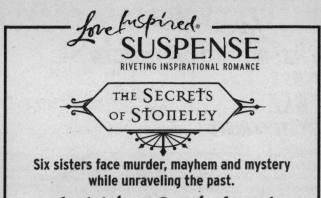
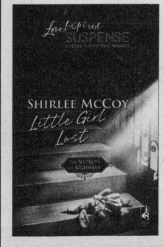

REQUEST YOUR FREE BOOKS!

2 FREE INSPIRATIONAL NOVELS
PLUS 2
FREE
MYSTERY GIFTS

Love Inspired®

YES! Please send me 2 FREE Love Inspired® novels and my 2 FREE mystery gifts. After receiving them, if I don't wish to receive any more books, I can return the shipping statement marked "cancel." If I don't cancel, I will receive 4 brand-new novels every month and be billed just $3.99 per book in the U.S., or $4.74 per book in Canada, plus 25¢ shipping and handling per book and applicable taxes, if any*. That's a savings of 20% off the cover price! I understand that accepting the 2 free books and gifts places me under no obligation to buy anything. I can always return a shipment and cancel at any time. Even if I never buy another book from Steeple Hill, the two free books and gifts are mine to keep forever.

113 IDN EF26 313 IDN EF27

Name	(PLEASE PRINT)	
Address		Apt. #
City	State/Prov.	Zip/Postal Code

Signature (if under 18, a parent or guardian must sign)

Order online at www.LoveInspiredBooks.com

Or mail to Steeple Hill Reader Service™:
IN U.S.A.: P.O. Box 1867, Buffalo, NY 14240-1867
IN CANADA: P.O. Box 609, Fort Erie, Ontario L2A 5X3

Not valid to current Love Inspired subscribers.

Want to try two free books from another series?
Call 1-800-873-8635 or visit www.morefreebooks.com

* Terms and prices subject to change without notice. NY residents add applicable sales tax. Canadian residents will be charged applicable provincial taxes and GST. This offer is limited to one order per household. All orders subject to approval. Credit or debit balances in a customer's account(s) may be offset by any other outstanding balance owed by or to the customer. Please allow 4 to 6 weeks for delivery.

LIREG07

Love Inspired

TITLES AVAILABLE NEXT MONTH

Don't miss these four stories in February

PRECIOUS BLESSINGS by Jillian Hart
The McKaslin Clan

His daughter a shoplifter? Jack Munroe didn't want to see the truth. Yet Katherine McKaslin, the bookstore's owner, certainly made him pay attention—and even consider a second chance at love.

THE SISTERHOOD OF THE DROPPED STITCHES
by Janet Tronstad
A special Steeple Hill Café novel in Love Inspired

Cancer survivor Marilee Davidson hadn't dated since her diagnosis, so she resolved to go on three dates. And when she put herself out there, she discovered love in the most unexpected of places.

HIS WINTER ROSE by Lois Richer
Serenity Bay

Piper Langley had no reason to trust her handsome new boss, Jason Franklin. But as she worked closely with the charming mayor of Serenity Bay, the ice around her jaded heart began to thaw.

DREAM A LITTLE DREAM by Debra Clopton

When reporter Molly Popp touted rancher Bob Jacobs's marriage worthiness, single women came running. Molly helped him fend them off, and fell for him in the process, forcing a choice between a big-city byline and a bachelor.

LICNM0107